D1579209

I'll survive even if it kills me

Ben MacGregor

With best wishes,

Ben MacGregor.

Curlew Cottage Books

Published by
Curlew Cottage Books
Curlew Cottage,
Hilliclay Mains,
Weydale, Thurso,
Caithness, KW14 8YN

ISBN 0-9538703-1-6

Typeset by
Whittles Publishing Services
Roseleigh House, Latheronwheel,
Caithness, KW5 6DW

Printed by The Print Register, Golspie

I'll survive even
if it kills me

Contents

If anyone has insight let him calculate the number of the beast, for it is man's number. His number is 666.

Preface

A book of short stories should, in my opinion, be fun to read. It should provide a means of escape from the often harsh realities of the real world. There is no reason why stories cannot embody some deeper truth or meaning – indeed there is more than you may at first think in this collection. A story's main purpose, however, should be to entertain, to hold the reader's attention and imagination. It is, after all, a *story*.

Much modern writing seems to have forgotten this. An author typically takes some dreadful human situation and explores all its repulsive ramifications. The writing, the portrayal of character and condition, may be excellent but is not the sort of thing I wish to read for relaxation. Nobody seems to be writing good, cracking tales any more.

So, in order to be able to read stories I liked, I had to write them myself. It then occurred to me that others might like them too. Hence this book. Many are ghost stories set in the modern world of computers and the Internet. A couple have a science-fiction background. Several take place in the Scottish Highlands where I live. Some of them involve the strange world of the Mandelbrot Set. If there is a common message behind the stories it is that there is far more to this universe than you have ever imagined. And, of course, that good is more powerful than evil.

'Connections', 'The MONK' and 'GPS' have appeared in the *John O' Groat Journal*. 'The fastest bathroom in the universe' was included in Kevin MacNeil's Highland compilation *A Little Borderless Village*. All the other stories are previously unpublished.

The tales and characters are purely fictional but many of the places are real. The stories do not explore the depths of the human condition. They are meant to be enjoyed. But beware if you start reading them on your own in the office on a dark winter afternoon. Never forget, computers can kill…

Ben MacGregor

The ghost in the machine

Haunted computers are no joke.

'Specialist computer systems investigator'. That's how I'm listed in the business directories. What I really do – well, that just gets round by word of mouth.

Remember the accident at the Red Point nuclear plant? Remember the subsequent sad death of Sandy Fraser? It was reckoned that severe stress had unhinged his mind. Sandy was not, however, mad. If he'd called me in to help he'd still be alive...

Until recently, genuine hauntings, poltergeists and the like had become increasingly rare, at least in the Western world. Modern technological advances and a sceptical scientific culture make things difficult for ghosts and evil spirits, in spite of a general decline in religious belief. The sheer numbers of people visiting haunted sites eventually erase all echoes of past events. People who die nowadays rarely have any intention of trying to return.

It has, however, been kept very quiet that there is a growing number of cases involving computer systems, and that is where I come in. Lynne J. Thomas – parapsychologist (to use a euphemism) and computer ghost-buster.

Advertising is tricky. I don't want publicity but it's important that the people who need me get to hear of my service. So my line is: when your system is playing up and the experts are baffled, call me. I only need to ask a few questions to ascertain if it's a real problem or not. Attempting to deal with a genuine attack without specialist knowledge can be extremely dangerous, as poor Sandy Fraser found out. Untreated, a business or entire organisation can be wrecked and there is a real danger that the problem can spread, like an evil cancer, across the network to other organisations. It's a bit like a simple computer virus but infinitely more dangerous. Even for me the work can involve considerable risk and can be spiritually and emotionally exhausting. So I don't come cheap.

The KAA case was one of the worst I've had to deal with. A high-technology, contract research outfit with a turnover of half a billion pounds a year and a couple of thousand employees is hardly the sort of place you might expect a good old-fashioned haunting…

Remember how the company was in trouble in the late '90s? It had been doing very well for a number of years, expanding business overseas and at home. Then something seemed to go wrong. Customer deadlines weren't being met. Budgets were exceeded. Acrimonious disputes arose on the board. The whole organisation became racked with infighting. There were stories of computer system problems, millions were spent on a new system but this failed to perform. Highly paid consultants came, and went.

Eventually somebody contacted me. The phone call took its familiar course. It happens less now; these days women are more accepted in the computer world.

'Hello, could I speak to Mr Thomas please?'

'MISS Thomas speaking, specialist computer investigator. Can I help you?'

'Yes. I wonder if could I make an appointment for Dr Bruce, head of IT at KAA plc, to meet Mr Thomas.'

'This is MISS Thomas, I run the business here. Could I speak to Dr Bruce?'

'I'm sorry, he's not in the office just now. Could I get him to call you later?'

Eventually I get to speak to somebody who knows about the

problem. There's usually a certain embarrassment on their part, a bit as if I'm a witch-doctor called in as a last resort when conventional medicine has failed. Well, I suppose I am, to some extent, and in many cases things have already been left far too long.

I don't know what people expect when I turn up, perhaps some old lady on a bike with a big black Bible and some sticks of incense. Instead – a top range red Porsche, a shapely blonde, neat suit, laptop computer, 3G mobile phone. Impressions are particularly important in my line.

As I walked into KAA head office I immediately felt uneasy. Women are, on the whole better than men at judging the feel of a place; the building – not the people, the building, definitely had an unfriendly feel to it.

The receptionist took my name and called Dr Bruce's office. Meanwhile I noticed that the PC on her desk, in screen saver mode, was behaving jerkily, as if a program was running in background. Images were moving across the screen, but every so often the screen froze for a fraction of a second. Then I saw, without any doubt at all, that for just an instant the flying windows moved BACKWARDS before returning to normal motion. Something was very wrong.

However it was when I walked into Dr Bruce's office that I really had a shock. Or rather two shocks. The first thing I noticed was a new, high-performance gigahertz machine on his desk from which emanated what you might call the psychic equivalent of a revolting smell. I always experience some feeling of revulsion when sitting down at the keyboard of a possessed machine but this one was so bad it seemed amazing that Dr Bruce was unaware of it. He got up to shake hands, and fortunately guided me over to a table for our discussions. I'd have found it impossible to sit at that desk for any length of time.

Already a little shaken, I'd hardly looked at Dr Bruce and now I had my second shock. I'd sort of expected your typical company computer manager but here was somebody who wouldn't have looked out of place in an Olympic stadium. Tall, young, a slim muscular build, a friendly smile. I'd meant to say: 'Good afternoon Dr Bruce. I'm Miss Thomas, specialist computer investigator.' Instead I found myself stuttering, 'Do you mind if I sit down...'

'Call me Jim,' he began, 'and you?'

'Lynne. Lynne Thomas.'

He was, as people always are, both apologetic and slightly embarrassed.

'Thank you very much for coming over. I hope this isn't a waste of your valuable time. We've had an ongoing problem with our computer systems and, well, we were advised that you may be able to help.'

He then proceeded to list the symptoms which had increasingly afflicted the company over the previous year. It was utterly obvious to me that my visit was long, long overdue. I only hoped that the problems had not been left to fester for so long that they were now terminal for the company.

There was initially a general slowness of the system and the network, but now even word-processors would seize up for ten minutes at a time. There was erratic performance of machines. Money was disappearing from financial systems, wrong invoices were sent, wrong bills were paid. Scientific calculations were giving plausible but dangerously wrong results. Errors were appearing, not at random but where they did serious damage, in project planning and in plant design. Confidential management and personnel information was being corrupted and would appear, seemingly at random, in people's mailboxes. Sordid details of employee's private lives were being mailed across the system. Spurious e-mail disclosing everything from personal information to malicious gossip to complete falsehoods kept appearing. Office relations had, as a result, deteriorated alarmingly. Everywhere there was infighting within the company. Work was grinding to a halt. The whole company was indeed on the verge of collapse.

'The new system seems to have only made things worse. None of the consultants have done any good at all. We've even tried isolating machines from the network but that makes no difference.'

'It wouldn't,' I said, 'you've got a real problem and I'm afraid it's pretty bad. You should have called me in long ago. I may be able to help but it might be too late for you. I'll need full support – from the top. I must have full authority from the Chief Executive to take any steps I deem necessary. You may lose data.'

'No problem! If we can't solve this soon, the company's sunk, we know that much. How much will you charge?'

'How many machines have you got?'

'Must be about 2000.'

'Well, my normal rate is £100 per machine. So £200K. But then if I don't succeed, nothing.' (I don't come cheap. But then I do have a Porsche to support.)

'That's more than I was expecting… OK.' He smiled, 'you're on.'

'Now,' I said, 'I must speak to the Chief Executive.'

Technical people frequently pour scorn on such things as possession by evil forces. Chief Executives usually have a broader background and are more amenable to the idea that such things still happen.

The CE was a worried man before I came to see him and even more so when I left. He'd not been properly briefed by his juniors and still thought that some technical solution was just around the corner. I explained as best as I could.

'Think of it like cancer. The evil gets into one machine. It spreads over the network to several others and grows there. It then spreads on to yet more machines. If it isn't halted, every machine in the network becomes infected with the evil force. It grows, steadily, taking up more of the machines' resources, more of the network. Its intelligence and power increase. Its only aim is to cause as much trouble, as much havoc, as much damage, as much pain as it can. If it can wreck lives, cause people to die, or be injured, it will. It's a devil, a true disembodied force of evil. Once it has taken root it can leap into machines which are not even networked. It can be extremely dangerous to fight. I've had years of experience of this kind of problem but your case looks as bad as I've seen. I can't promise to succeed but I'll do my best. I must however have your full support, your full authority. I must have access to all computer systems and data. I must have complete freedom to take any action required. Some of my techniques may appear unconventional but you must trust me.'

'You're our last hope. I don't have much choice. But are you quite certain that it's not just a simple virus?'

I had to take a slight risk, I didn't want to frighten the poor man too much and give him a heart attack, but had to get the message across.

'Look. Let me show you.' I sat down at the keyboard of his PC. My skin crawled as I reached for the keys of the revolting machine. My body shuddered as if hearing steel screech off stone. I could feel the slimy, cold force of malice emanating from the central processor. I couldn't do this work without a strong religious faith, if I didn't know that the forces of good were more powerful.

I steeled myself and clicked the mouse a couple of times to open a new file on the word processor. 'Just read that,' I said.

'F— OFF F— OFF GET OFF THIS MACHINE! GET OFF YOU – - – bitch, get back to the midden where you came from, all Thomases will burn in hell for evermore if you don't leave NOW. We'll get you tonight, we'll …' and so on, going into graphic detail of what 'they' would do to me, what they thought of me and my family, using the most insulting and obscene language and descriptions.

I'm fairly used to this sort of thing but it still comes as a bit of a shock. The poor chief executive was meanwhile frantically clicking the mouse to try and quit the program.

'It won't work, I'm afraid,' I said. 'There's only one thing to do.'

I picked up a pencil from the desk and used it to turn the power switch off.

'If there was any fault at all in the earthing, it would try and electrocute me,' I explained.

He looked a bit white. 'I'm sorry I didn't believe you. I'm sure you're genuine. But there are still some powerful people in this company who don't. I'm sorry – but – there are some who know the kind of work you do and say, well, that it's all a racket, that you hack into computer systems, cause havoc and then charge a fortune for putting right your own damage. How can I convince them?'

'Don't worry, it's a charge that's often levelled against me! You can only convince the doubters if you yourself believe that I'm genuine. Firstly I'm a Christian. It would be contrary to my faith to deceive on such a scale. Secondly, if I really were in league with the forces that are wrecking your organisation I could gain a lot more by working with them, by smashing you to pieces then buying up the wreckage. Thirdly, if the problem were caused by ordinary computer viruses, or similar, it would have been sorted by now, you've certainly had enough computer experts crawling over the system! If you're feeling strong, you can watch me have a go now at cleaning up at least your machine.'

'By all means, if you can.'

'First I must unplug it from the network.'

I pulled the Ethernet socket out of the back of the machine.

'Next I connect it to my own portable which is protected and immune to any attack, it will feed its own agents into your machine and, in effect, carry out an exorcism.'

As I was speaking I booted up my own machine and connected the two together using a short length of Ethernet cable. Then I powered up the other machine, launched my software and waited. It's a procedure I've followed many times. Often there is an audible wail, or a scream, or a mutter of curses, then after a minute or so the clean desktop appears and I can immediately feel that the machine is wholesome again. Occasionally however things are not quite so simple, and this was one of those occasions. On the screen of my machine a message appeared WARNING OVERLOAD DUMPING PROGRAM. From the other machine came the most hellish yell imaginable, a spine-chilling, neck-crawling yowl of sheer hate. The screen went red and yellow, displaying vile and revolting images of naked humans undergoing torture. I could feel the hate pulsating outwards. I had to take drastic measures. 'In the name of the Father, the Son and the Holy Ghost,' I shouted, 'begone and never return.' There was a scream. A bang. The screen shattered. Smoke billowed out.

'Get the fire extinguisher!' I shouted. Then the fire alarms went off.

An hour later, when everyone had returned to the building after the evacuation, we sat with a couple of cups of strong coffee in an adjoining lounge. Most of these top people are tough, they have to be to get there.

'I'm sorry,' I said. 'I didn't intend to ruin your machine. I didn't realise quite how serious the problem was!'

'Neither did I! Are you sure its not incurable?'

'The computer system problem is curable all right. Whether your organisation can recover or not – well, that one's up to you. I'm afraid however that I'll need help, its more than I can manage alone. I'll need to bring in somebody from the States. It'll put the price up as he'll also want a couple of hundred K...'

'Don't worry. Half a million if you can clear the problem within four weeks and give us a guarantee.'

One thing about these these top people is that they're good at quick decisions.

'Four weeks... OK. Done.' We shook hands. 'Now I need to know a bit more about the history of this place...'

I wasted no time in phoning up Don, a freelance computer system consultant in Oregon. I've known Don for many years, just good friends, you understand. Don is a rare example of an extreme reductionist, logician and atheist. He's also a really nice guy who wouldn't hurt a fly and would go far further in obeying the teaching of the Sermon on the Mount than most who claim to be Christians.

Don simply refuses to believe that anything in this world is other than a direct consequence of the outworking of physical laws in our bodies and environments. His religion is that God doesn't exist, nor do ghosts, evil spirits, the Devil or anything else of that ilk. Why is the universe here? A meaningless question to him so no point in asking. The universe is nothing other than matter, energy, mathematics and the resultant outworkings thereof.

Of course, powers of evil can do little to harm or influence anyone who refuses to acknowledge that they exist! Don and I get on remarkably well when there's a really tough assignment.

I explained the problem to him over the phone and mentioned the offered sum of half a million if we could sort it out. His reply was just what I'd expected, 'I keep telling you. There's nothing mysterious about computer systems. All your stuff about possession and evil forces is just imagination. There's nothing more going on than a slight perturbation in the pattern of electrons moving through simple circuit components It's just some cunning virus or worm written by a simple-minded programmer; you can always clear these things if you get right back to system assembler code. I'll be over on Saturday!'

I reckoned I might be able to deal with the haunting, which is really what it was, but could only do so by destroying all the computers. KAA would not be pleased. To deal with machines individually – well I simply did not have the strength for that, whatever supernatural assistance I might be able to call on. Now Don – the computer could be simply crawling with slimy, evil nasties and he wouldn't even notice. So if I could isolate the 'thing' – demon, ghost, spirit – call it what you will – he could deal with it as a bit of unwanted electrical activity. He needed ME so that he could clean up the computers without erasing all the data. I needed HIM so that the evil could be eradicated without destroying the machines. Yet each of us was totally convinced that the other had the wrong idea as to what the real problem was.

As we drove into KAA on Monday we had our usual banter.

'I think I've sussed the problem,' I told Don. 'When the HQ

was being built, some large stones were unearthed. They did some emergency archaeology and discovered that the site had been extensively used over thousands of years. There was an almost complete stone circle. There was layer upon layer of charcoal containing bone fragments subsequently found to be mostly human. Several ornate knife-handles and sharp flints were uncovered. Some complete bones had knife marks indicating de-fleshing of bones and, more interestingly, human tooth marks. It would appear that it was a site of ritual cannibalism, and the carbon-dating showed that the site had been used for that purpose from at least 2000BC until only a few hundred years ago. It was then in the heart of the forest and quite a remote spot...'

Don interjected, 'So you're saying that some kind of evil spirit has hung around since then and now taken up residence in the computers? Where was it living in the meantime if it needs the electronics? What could possibly attract a ghost to a load of PCs? I'm sure that, if you looked into it, somebody has died or been killed in just about every hectare of this country at some time or other. Where are all the ghosts? It really is about time we forgot all that silly superstition!'

'Superstition? It's no such thing!' I replied. 'People in the past were closer to the spiritual world, it's just that all our modern technology keeps us from thinking and drowns out its influence, giving us the illusion that this material world is all there is! My great great grandmother was burnt at the stake for what she did, not because of superstition!'

'MY grandparents were killed at Belsen,' replied Don, 'that wasn't superstition either. There will always be bad people in this world, out for their own ends, who can have influence over others. But everything, good or bad, only comes from people. There is absolutely no need or indeed evidence of any kind to suggest there is anything more than that!'

'Look,' I replied, 'whatever your beliefs, you can't get away from the facts. I drove SOMETHING out of that chief executive's computer which caused it to blow up! Besides, how come that computers which aren't even networked are affected?'

'I'm not saying that there isn't SOMETHING there,' countered Don. 'But even I could write a virus in half a day that would produce most of the effects you describe. All you need is a few people with inside knowledge trying to wreck the company. It's easy to infect an apparently isolated machine either just by sneaking in a disc or by downloading a virus through the infrared port. As for blowing up the machine, that could easily be rigged up by tapping into the mains and sending a surge of power at the right moment. Somebody will have been sitting in another office, watching and listening to everything that was going on through a hidden video camera!'

'It all sounds pretty far-fetched to me; my explanation is much the simpler,' I replied. 'Besides, how do you explain that those infected machines – well – stank, even before I knew there was a bad problem?'

'Easy,' said Don. 'I don't suppose you'd agree that it's all in your imagination so I suspect a low-frequency infra-sound signal coupled with a certain choice of clashing colours and asymmetrical positioning which would immediately be picked up by the subconscious of a sensitive person like you...'

'Thank you,' I replied, 'I suppose that was meant as a back-handed compliment. But you can explain anything away if you want to. And you and I are just a complex bit of chemistry and electronics?'

'Add software to that,' replied Don, 'and yes, of course – what else?'

So, it was the unlikely team of a Christian white witch and a scientific atheist who arrived at eight on an ordinary grey Monday morning to sort out the KAA computer network. The company had by now almost stopped working. A directive banning the use of all computers had been issued. Unfortunately nobody could work without them. There were no typewriters. No paper stock control or accounts systems. No paper purchasing system. Computer aided design systems were needed for design work. Assessment work needed computer calculations. Experimental work needed computer control. Not even bank transfers of employees' salaries could be made. Staff were already being laid off. The computers sat sullen and silent. Whatever Don might think, I didn't like the feel of them, even switched off.

We decided to make a start with Jim Bruce's machine. We disconnected it from the network and I let Don switch it on and boot it up.

'I'll put a metal screen round it,' said Don, 'that will make sure that nobody is monitoring or interfering with it from outside.'

'If you like,' I replied, 'but if you don't mind, I'll draw a chalk circle around it to keep out the kind of outside influence I think is causing the problems...'

We work well together.

I could feel waves of hate emanating from the machine but Don was completely oblivious, already deep into the system. 'Problem seems to be in the main processor. There are a number of active tasks drawing power away from the main system control. I wonder, could you shift the virus onto the hard drive for me?'

'Right,' I said. 'Lets go!'

I plugged in my portable and initiated the program in a mode which should clear the main processors and memory. Once again the screen flickered with lurid images, but gradually a gentle blue-white glow grew from the top left, pushing the violent nastinesses to the bottom right-hand corner where they stayed, pulsating and writhing. It makes my skin crawl to even think of it. I was only too glad to hand the machine back to Don.

'Nice software you've got there,' he said. 'Pity it doesn't work with me. Saves me a lot of time though...Hmm, definitely nasty, a lot of the disk is being actively accessed; we need to be careful not to wipe the data. Now let me load up my own software assembler code which cancels every active process accessing the hard drive...'

It worked, it always did. The images died away. The screen cleared. I could feel immediately that the machine was wholesome. Don, however, needed a more rigorous check and ran through the whole system. 'Clever things, some of these viruses, can hide even on a clock chip. One done, 1999 to go!'

Things were not however going to be so easy.

Now we reckoned we'd bottomed the problem we thought we'd try and clear machines over the network rather than deal with them tediously, one at a time.

We used belt and braces to make sure that Jim Bruce's machine wasn't reinfected, the belt being my 'GARLIC' software, which Don reckoned was a complete waste of time; the braces being his immune-system anti-virus suite which I knew was just a waste of hard disc space. We reconnected the machine to the network and started trying to work outwards, the idea being to create successive rings of clean machines.

At first, things seemed to be working, we cleaned a couple of machines but then it was like hitting a wall. Nothing I could do would get any further, there was some utterly solid evil force barring any further progress. Never before had I encountered such opposition. Don, too, could simply not get sufficient access to investigate further. We identified the problem network node and switched off.

Jim Bruce was puzzled when we explained the problem to him. 'That machine doesn't exist any more. We replaced it a couple of years ago. It kept playing up but we couldn't find anything wrong with it and since it was only an old 586 we simply scrapped it. With hindsight, that was the beginning of our problems.'

'So where is it now?' I asked.

'Oh it'll be sitting around on top of some filing cabinet gathering dust. It was never thrown out because a few people expressed an interest in buying it but these things take such a lot of bureaucracy in this firm and I never got round to sorting out the paperwork.'

'Could you find it for us, please,' said Don, 'it might save us a lot of hassle.'

The following day we went in as before and asked to see Dr Bruce. The receptionist didn't seem to know what to say. 'It's OK,' I said, 'we'll wait till he's free.'

'Haven't you heard?' she finally blurted out. 'He was found last night – dead – it's horrible...' and she burst into tears. 'I'm sorry,' I said, 'we didn't realise...'

I felt sick. And very angry. 'Damn and blast, what were we thinking of in putting Jim into such danger. Things are really bad.'

'Danger?' Don was puzzled. 'I just asked him to find a computer! But this is terrible. I suppose the police will be involved.'

'Well, we'd better find out what happened,' I replied wearily. I went back to the desk where the poor girl was still sobbing. 'I'm sorry, but we must see the Chief Executive.'

The CE agreed to see us immediately. He looked shocked and white. He asked us to sit down and warned us that the story was not nice.

'It appears to have been a nasty accident. The police are investigating but it doesn't look like there were any suspicious circumstances. It seems that Jim was trying to get a computer and screen down from the top of a filing cabinet in the basement of the finance building when he slipped and fell awkwardly, dragging both the filing cabinet and the computer equipment on top of him. His back was broken and he was pinned against a radiator. Coincidentally a fault had just developed in the heating in that building and the radiator was too hot, perhaps 70°C. He was slowly cooked. The horrible thing is that he was probably fully conscious till the end. The pain must have been terrible. He was in the building after normal office hours and there was nobody to hear his cries. When people went in this morning there was a smell...'

Don and I looked at each other.

'Now,' I said, 'do you believe this is more than just a virus?'

'A freak accident,' said Don, 'terrible but – just a freak accident.'

'As soon as you can,' I said to the CE, 'you must let us see where this happened and in particular we must see that computer.'

The next day, when the body of poor Jim Bruce had been removed and the police had gone, we were allowed into that accursed basement. The Chief Executive himself took us down but just as we were entering the building his mobile phone rang. It was an urgent message, an important overseas customer had arrived on site half an hour early and was waiting to see him. I told him it would be fine to leave us on our own. I should have known better.

I already knew that this was a particularly nasty problem but as we went down the stairs into the basement the sense of evil became almost overpowering. Don was, as usual, completely oblivious and before I could manage to warn him, walked calmly up to an old 586 computer and screen, now sitting on a desk. 'Wait,' I said, weakly, but he was already plugging the machine in and switching it on, 'WAIT'. I tried to shout but the sense of evil was so strong I could hardly more than whisper. This could be too much for both of us.

'Seems to be working still,' said Don, 'now lets have a look at the system – AAAGGHH.' He screamed. His hand was clenched on the mouse.

'Live...electrocute...Swiiitchh oooofffff...' I tried to move towards the power socket but there was something almost physically stopping me. I couldn't make any progress. Don was writhing in the agony of electrocution. The PC toppled off the desk and hit the floor. I was blacking out. Pray I thought desperately PRAY – but my mind had gone and I couldn't think...

Then suddenly there was another presence in the room.

I felt, rather than heard the words. 'Get back you stupid demon. You're not getting away with another victim. You got me but now I'm going to get YOU!' It was Jim Bruce's voice! 'I don't care if you've all the powers of Hell at your disposal, You're NOT getting away with this. There was a cackling laugh cut off suddenly in a scream and a thud. 'Thought you'd won, did you. Well I wasn't the number two Karate in Britain for nothing! Take that, and that, and that – and if I have to chase you to the

Hell you came from I'll do the same to your masters!'

Suddenly I realised I was free to move. I crawled to the mains socket and pulled out the plug. Don – was it too late – no, he was breathing. He opened his eyes. He was sweating. 'Phew. You got to the socket then. How could I be so stupid…Thanks …Thanks.'

'Thanks,' I said, 'to Jim…'

'JIM??'

'The first thing we do now,' I said wearily, 'is smash this machine into little pieces…'

After that, dealing with the rest of the problem was an anticlimax. The network was free again. Don's specialist anti-virus software cleaned most of the machines overnight, it just needed a little help from me to deal with a few more stubborn ones but resistance was almost non-existent. Within three days the entire company was clean. Or almost.

We'd been working from the computer in Jim Bruce's office. Don was puzzled. 'It's odd but there's still something not quite right with this machine. There's a spurious process going on somewhere but I just can't track it down.'

'There's nothing wrong with that machine,' I said, 'I know!'

Indeed the machine now seemed to have a positively friendly feel to it.

'I wonder,' I said. 'Give me the keyboard.' I logged myself onto the system. Immediately there was a beep, an item of e-mail for me. I clicked on it. The message was new, it had just been sent.

'Sorry we never met outside work. Maybe some other time… I'll just stick around here for a while longer and make sure everything stays OK. Thanks, and don't forget to collect your pay cheque! Yours, Jim Bruce.'

I pressed the delete button before Don could read it.

'Nothing wrong with that machine,' I said. 'Must be a bug in your software!'

The MONK

I haven't long to live. At most a couple of hours before I'll be capable of nothing more than screaming in agony and lapsing into unconsciousness. Nobody can do anything for me now. I can still type into my computer though, and there's just enough time left to write my account of what really happened at Red Point...

I've been a criticality safety specialist at the Red Point nuclear reprocessing plant for the last 20 years. The plant handles lots of plutonium and we have to make sure that nothing goes critical by accident – there'd be no atomic explosion but there would be a huge burst of radiation which would kill anybody nearby. My job's been to lead the team which advises plant managers and designers on how to make sure that their equipment is always safe. It's usually a pretty routine job but once in a while there's an interesting problem.

I'd been away for three weeks on a late Autumn holiday, longer than usual, and had left two experienced team members, Mary and Mike, holding the fort. Apart from some ongoing long-term assessment work, we didn't expect anything other than routine enquiries. So I was surprised to hear what Mike had to tell me when I got back.

'We've been rushed off our feet. Quite a panic, in fact almost like old times!' The plant used to do a lot of government work and there would always be unrealistic edicts coming down from on high that some bit of kit had to be working by Monday. Leave would be cancelled, overtime worked and weekends sacrificed but, inevitably, it would be three months before the plant actually started up.

I asked what had been going on.

'Seems that there was a very lucrative contract for the Germans if the fuel could be taken onto site, reprocessed and returned all within four weeks. They've been going flat out to refurbish the old dissolver in R2201 and of course we had only a fortnight to do the criticality assessment!'

'Glad I was away,' I said, meaning it. 'So it's all finished and written up?'

'Yes, had to get it through the system, peer review and all. We've just issued the criticality clearance certificates and the plant, believe it or not, is due to start up today!'

'Do you think I should have a look at the assessment?' I asked, knowing full well that I should, but not wanting to sound as if I didn't trust Mary and Mike. Good solid workers, both of them, but not experienced at dealing with unusual problems.

'Actually we'd be very pleased if you did,' said Mike. 'We had to do the MONKs in a hurry and some of the reactivities were only just below 0.95. They've all been checked but another look-over would do no harm.'

'MONK' is one of those dreadful acronyms dreamed up by unimaginative physicists. It starts for "Monte-Carlo Criticality", "Monte-Carlo" being another whimsical name for a computer method which uses random numbers, rather like throwing dice, to simulate random processes, in this instance those of nuclear fission. We use the MONK computer code a lot, it allows us to set up computer models of complex plant and see how close to critical they are. The code calculates a number, the so-called reactivity, which is a measure of this. A value of 1 is critical, 0.8 is 80% critical and so on.

The refurbished plant was indeed fairly complex. Dissolvers tend to be messy in construction but this one was particularly awkward, a star of interconnecting pipes. Mary had done pretty well in getting the MONK computer model of the dissolver set up so quickly. All the quality assurance documentation seemed to be in place. The plant had been measured to confirm it checked with the drawings, the calculational data had been checked, the assessment had been peer-reviewed by an outside consultant then accepted by the site safety committee.

Some questions had been asked as the plant could be closer to critical than was usually permitted. I too had some niggling doubts, the curves of reactivity against concentration looked flatter than I'd have expected and maybe the convergence could have been better but I couldn't find anything wrong with the input data.

'It's a good thing we bought the new computer,' said Mary, 'it runs MONK about three times faster than before and we'd never have got all the runs done in time otherwise.'

'I hope you checked the validation cases first!' was my reply – the set of test cases which should always be run on a new machine to ensure it is performing properly.

'Yes,' Mary said, 'we've put them all through, no problem at all.'

'Looks like a good job done then,' I replied, 'I'll have to go on holiday more often!'

That night came the 2am phone call. The thing I'd always dreaded since taking on the job of criticality safety officer. 'Shift manager here. We've had a criticality accident in R2201. We need your advice. Could you come into site and report to the emergency control centre please.'

'Are you sure it's not just a false alarm?' I asked, hoping I might still get a night's sleep.

'I'm afraid this one's real. Surveys have shown high radiation levels in R2201 and poor Davie Fraser's in a bad way, seems he was right next to the dissolver when it went...'

The refurbished dissolver! As I drove towards site on the dark, empty roads through the December gale I tried to imagine how the accident could have occurred. Surely we'd identified all possibilities and shown that there was no hazard.

The first thing to do was to shut the reaction down, the dissolver was still boiling away in a critical state just like a little reactor. That was easy, just use the installed remotely operated transfer system to pump liquor into safe tanks. There had been no spread of contamination so clean-up was going to be a minor problem. The main thing was to try to understand what had gone wrong.

The dissolver had apparently been running entirely routinely and was about two-thirds way through dissolving a batch of the German plutonium. Davie had approached to check the wiring to a failed level gauge and it seems that the increased reflection of neutrons from his body may have triggered the accident. He'd had a massive dose of radiation and had now lapsed into a coma. He'd live for another day or two at most, poor man. One or two other workers had received significant, but not lethal, radiation doses.

'There's one thing perhaps you should know,' said the incident controller, 'that may have a bearing on the accident. Before he went unconscious poor Davie was heard moaning "the MONK, the MONK".'

As we all know, the accident made headlines across the world. The new plant would be shut down until the cause was known, and perhaps for good.... Our team came under a lot of pressure, which grew as the evidence came in that the dissolver had been running entirely as designed.

Davie's last words really bothered me. A good lad, Davie, but not into nuclear physics – so why was he apparently worried about our calculations? I decided to set up a new computer model of the plant myself and redo the key runs. I worked all the next day and late into the evening and it was with some relief that I saw that my model was giving the same results as Mary's. So what was wrong? The next thing was to double-check the plant dimensions; as soon as radiation levels were low enough we went in and remeasured the plant, all was fine. The plutonium isotopics were checked, sampled, rechecked – again no problem.

We had to be sure that the accident had nothing to do with

our MONK calculations. I was trying variations in the key run to see if there was any unusual sensitivity to isotopics and by mistake ran a case on one of the older, slower computers. The predicted reactivity came out critical at 1.01. I repeated the base case. Again a critical reactivity of 1.02.

The calculations, when run on the older computers, predicted that the dissolver would be critical under normal operations.

I double-checked the data. I ran the same input deck simultaneously on three different machines. The new computer still predicted that the dissolver was safely sub-critical at 0.94. Both old computers however said it was critical at 1.02.

It's not nice to know you've killed someone because of a computer fault.

The first thing we did was recheck all the validation cases on the new computer. They ran fine. We reran other cases. They also gave the right results on the new machine. The new computer gave the wrong answer, showing a safe margin from criticality, *only when used for the new dissolver.*

I'd heard of an instance, once before, where a MONK result varied slightly depending on the time of day when the case was run. That had been traced to a temperature-sensitive computer chip. We contacted the computer supplier and explained the problem. Never has an engineer been so speedily dispatched, he was on site that day and installed a new mother-board. It made no difference.

That night, leaving late, I heard faint peels of laughter coming out of the locked office where the machine was housed. Hysterical, female laughter. I groaned. The old cuckoo-clock problem must have resurfaced, presumably with all the messing around with the boards. Let me explain. A few years ago there was a big reorganisation and we inherited computers from a group which had disbanded. These folk, for some odd reason, had set their machines to sound like cuckoo-clocks every hour. So come 12 noon and all the machines would let of a chorus of 12 'cuckoos'.

To remove the irritating cuckoos was not as easy as you might think, I had to study manuals describing obscure bits of the operating system before managing to silence most of them. One or two proved particularly tricky and I was driven to the crude approach of replacing the 'cuckoo' by a 'silent' sound. We'd been lax about changing passwords and some joker from the old group logged onto one of our machines over the network. Noticing my crude 'patch' he replaced my 'silent' sound by one giving bursts of hysterical female laughter then buried this deep in the system.

So we had a machine which, every hour, burst into peels of laughter. We put it in an empty office till we had time to sort the problem out and made sure that we changed all the passwords. One day there was a meeting of high-ups and one of them asked for an empty office to make some phone calls. He was, apparently, on the line to the Chairman when the computer on his desk burst into twelve howls of hysterical female laughter...

So, somehow, the cuckoo-clock problem had resurfaced on our new machine. Odd, though, that the time wasn't on the hour. But it did suggest that we might have a network problem, perhaps a virus... We took the new machine off the network. We wiped all the discs clean. We installed afresh all the software, we installed a new version of MONK. We now had an isolated, stand-alone machine. We ran the MONK case for the new-dissolver and still the answer came out too low. At least the laughter seemed to have stopped...

As Section Head I felt the responsibility keenly. I wasn't sleeping much. I couldn't get the problem out of my mind so came in again late yesterday evening to try and finally sort it out. I've always been one of those people who function best late at night and had more or less decided that if I didn't get the problem solved by the morning I'd resign from the job. Heads must roll somewhere when somebody gets killed.

The urgency of the contract meant that the plant management had decided to cut their losses and start using an older, neighbouring, dissolver instead even though throughputs were much lower and other work had to stop. There was no problem with the criticality safety of this one, it had been cleared in the past for all concentrations and isotopics, though it had never actually run with the more reactive fuel currently going through. It had been re-assessed only recently, not long after we bought the new computer.

It occurred to me that it mightn't be a bad idea to have a look at the recent assessment for the old dissolver, perhaps there would be some hints there. I got the file out and soon noticed that some key items of quality assurance were missing; there were no drawings or records of checks of plant dimensions. The models all used 100mm diameter pipework but I seemed to recall that the pipes were bigger. The plant had been running safely for years, but never before with such reactive fuel. I thought I'd better just confirm the pipe diameter used in the MONK computer models. Now was as good a time as any. I phoned the shift manager. 'Fine, we're just about to change over to night-shift but come across any time...'

I'd never actually been into the plants outside normal working hours and found them strangely quiet. In R2201 there was only a small night-shift team which had just arrived, and the supervisor left me to walk on my own down to the dissolver area. It was midnight on Friday 21st December.

As I'd feared, the dissolver pipework looked a lot bigger than 100mm diameter. I got my tape measure out and squeezed up against the main limb of the dissolver to measure the circumference.

There was a brilliant blue flash.

The dissolver had gone critical.

And, silhouetted against the blue, was a great, dark, figure of a hooded monk, his face a grin of gleeful and devilish malice. Next thing the criticality alarms were screaming, get out, get out, get out...

I was a dead man. I walked over to the manual control panel and pressed the buttons to empty the dissolver and shut the chain reaction down. I remembered poor Davie's last words.

Now I understood. Suddenly I was violently sick. I must have had a huge dose of radiation. I'd have perhaps an hour or two while I could still function...

I left the plant by the back door and walked across the dark site to my office. The site alert was now sounding, sirens wailing out into the black December night. I'd be accounted as missing but it would be hours before anyone would try and re-enter the plant. I had just time to get the true story out.

The new computer was laughing hysterically as I passed the office in which it sat, but the tone had changed to an evil cackle. I ignored it. I sat down at my machine and began to type.

Davie Fraser was the man who died in the first accident. I'm a Fraser too. When the Red Point plant was built, in the '50s, the remains of ancient stone foundations were found. It was conjectured that this was the site of an old monastery, long destroyed, about which legends still lingered.

According to the stories, the monks, mostly Camerons, were not over-religious and were in cahoots with the clan chief who was very much a man of his time. Under the protection of the monastery the Camerons stored up ill-gotten gains from smuggling, from luring ships onto the rocky coastline and from raids and feuds with the neighbouring Frasers. As would happen with clan skirmishes, tit-for-tat escalated till one wild night in late December the Frasers descended on the monastery and sacked it. Most of the so-called monks were killed in the fighting or escaped but a couple were captured alive and subjected to torture to reveal the whereabouts of what the Frasers believed were vast accumulated treasures. It is said that they never yielded, and the last one died by being slowly roasted over a smouldering fire while the Frasers laughed and joked. As he died he called out a curse that any Fraser who set foot on that spot in future would likewise die in a slow fire.

The treasure, if it ever existed, was never found. From then on, no Fraser would cross Red Point in December, a superstition which still persisted at the time when the plant was built...

Something evil had got into the new computer. It affected

the MONK computer calculations so that the new plant looked safe. It changed the dimensions of the old plant on the MONK computer model to make it look safe with the new fuel.

Already my skin feels as if it is burning all over; the pain will soon be unbearable. My head is exploding. Radiation overdose is not a nice way to go. I'm going to e-mail this account to the main newspapers then I'm going into the office next door with the new computer, I'll lock the door, make a pile of papers and set light to it...

Click 37 and die

It was, I should have realised, more than a coincidence that two Durham University maths lecturers should die of heart attacks in the same fortnight.

I'd spent a happy four years at Durham but had never been back in the following fifteen. Pastures new had beckoned and I'd actually been quite glad to see the back of the place. Now I knew hardly anyone there, except for an old professor who still sent me a Christmas card every year.

The last thing I was expecting was a phone call from my old department where I'd done an MSc in pure maths. (What can you do with an MSc in pure maths? That's one reason I ended up in a branch of what you might call the old family business!) I could tell immediately that it wasn't the usual call from some big organisation. The secretary had my name right ('Is that Miss Lynne Thomas?') and Professor Rendall was waiting on the line to speak to me there and then. Professor Rendall! Must be nearing retiring age, I thought – and nearly 15 years since I last spoke to him. What on earth could he want?

'I don't know if you remember me,' he began, 'you worked under me as an MSc student in 1984.'

'I remember you fine,' I replied. 'How are you doing? You didn't become a ski instructor then?' (One of the maths lecturers at the time had caused a stir by disappearing off to Austria with somebody else's wife to start a ski school.)

'No, but I often wish I had! Too much administration and not enough work these days. Nothing but one funding crisis after another. Anyway what I really wanted to ask you is – would you be able to help us out with a problem?'

'Possibly,' I replied in my usual non-committal way, 'it depends on how much work's required, or indeed whether I can help at all. What's involved?'

'It's rather serious, and rather sensitive. I'd prefer not talk on the phone. Would you be able to come over? We'll pay your travel expenses of course!'

Travel expenses. That's universities for you. Normally I'd be charging at least £500 a day. But then it was my old department, and it would be nice to go back. I agreed to an appointment in a couple of days time.

I drove over the Pennines on a fine April day of cumulus cloud and long views, streaks of snow still near the summit of Mickle Fell and Cross Fell. All those roads I used to cycle as a student – yes, I'd get the bike out again when this trip was over! Lambing was in full swing, battered landrovers and dusty pickups were virtually the only other vehicles on the roads through Teesdale and my red Porsche turned quite a few heads.

I'm used to driving up to plush company headquarters where a smart sports car gives just the right image. It was a strange contrast to turn off the main road into the University Science Site and park amidst an array of old Escorts and Cortinas next to an ancient VW Beetle. My natty business-woman's outfit certainly commanded attention at the reception desk but made me feel very conspicuous in a building where jeans and a sweater or open-necked shirt were the norm. I'd been too long in the business world.

Professor Rendall had always been a bit of an exception in wearing a shirt and tie, so I felt a bit less out of place when I was ushered into his office. He didn't seem to have aged at all since I'd last seen him. We shook hands.

Once again the contrast with the big companies struck me. Any senior executive would have had a huge plush desk equipped with high-performance computer and phone but nothing else on acres of polished leather other than a note-pad. Here was an old wooden bureau, probably dating from when the department was built. The actual surface of the desk was invisible beneath piles of books and papers, some high enough to have reached the tottering stage. A small space had been cleared in front of where the professor sat. There wasn't a computer in sight.

'I'm very pleased you agreed to come over,' Professor Rendall began. 'We need your advice.'

'Before we begin, Professor,' I replied, 'you are aware of my field of work?'

'Specialist computer advisor – at least that's what you call yourself. But we always maintain a close interest in our old students so I've a pretty good idea of what you really do. And we've a situation here where, well, you may or may not be able to help, but if you can't we'll at least have eliminated one possibility. By the way, call me Alan.'

'And I'm Lynne. You use a computer yourself?'

'Never learnt to drive one of the things I'm afraid. One advantage of my branch of pure maths is that you only need a blackboard and chalk! But there are plenty of computers in the department, and that's where you may be able to help.'

'Coming to the point – what's your problem then?'

'You'll understand that this is all strictly confidential of course...'

I replied that I always respected clients' confidentiality and was security vetted to the highest level.

Alan was still obviously uncomfortable. 'I don't know whether you remember Michael Taylor?'

'He was the one who went off to start a ski school, wasn't he?'

'That's right – with Don Stephenson's wife! Caused quite a scandal in the late 1970s. He was carrying out research on fractals, indeed he was well ahead of his time and had recognised the potential of computers long before Mandelbrot. It always struck us as strange that he should suddenly break off and disappear

28

like a drop-out when he was in the middle of some very successful work.'

'What's he doing now?'

'Dead, I'm afraid. We were trying to contact him and discovered that he'd had a heart attack – at any rate that was the diagnosis – just two weeks earlier. He was getting too old for ski-instructing and had recently returned to mathematics. They reckoned it was the change to a sedentary existence that did it but I'm not so sure. You've probably heard that we've had two deaths in this department in the last fortnight. Both heart attacks.'

'I'm sorry...'

'Yes. Both colleagues of many years. Dr John Scriven and Dr Mary Booth. Both excellent mathematicians. As you can imagine the department is in something of a state of shock. It's not good for the students, either, who'll be back next week.'

'But – heart attacks – I hope you don't mind me asking – surely nothing suspicious?'

'No. At least not as far as the police or doctors are concerned. Both were found slumped in front of their computers. Not suicide, either, they're sure of that. Besides I knew them both very well, they were normal, well-adjusted people, no special problems or difficulties beyond what any of us have to face in life.'

'So why do you need my help?'

Alan Rendall sighed. 'You probably know that I'm a Christian. All three of the people we've been talking about were that rare breed – convinced atheist. Many's the debate I've had with all of them! All three were doing research in the same branch of fractal theory. To me, well, I may be wrong but I smell evil. You have experience of dealing with such things, perhaps at least you can put my mind at rest and assure me it's nothing but a chance stochastic cluster!'

'My specialism is with computers. If it's more general than that, I'm not really the right person...'

'We've now had three people dead in front of their machines. All Durham or ex-Durham. All atheists. All researching on fractal theory. The computers are the most likely link, if there is one.'

'Could I see the computers that John and Mary were using? I should be able to tell immediately if there's anything obvious.'

'No problem! I've been keeping others from using them in the meantime, just in case.'

We walked down the corridor into a large hall, a central space with easy chairs where several men and women were gathered in front of a blackboard. There was a surrounding walkway with offices opening off it.

'This is how we do maths these days,' explained the professor. 'Interaction with others is essential to the creative mathematical process. All offices have open doors, anyone at any time can come and make a cup of coffee, have a discussion with anyone else from the department. It always used to be true that the best work was done over tea-break, so we've extended the tea-break to last the whole day!'

We walked past the coffee machines and a soft-drinks dispenser and turned into one of the open offices. 'This is Mary's. It's much as she left it.'

The desk was tidy, with a small PC and phone.

'Not a very powerful computer?'

'They're all networked to the University CRAY cluster. Anything which needs any power uses the mainframe. The local machines are just used for things like word-processing.'

I didn't say anything but knew then that, if there was a problem, the whole university would be infected.

'I suppose we'll have to get Mary's stuff tidied out...' Alan pulled open a desk drawer which contained a very black banana, a half-eaten Muesli bar and a copy of *New Scientist*. 'It always seemed to happen when you came in here that she'd be eating a banana and reading a magazine, but she did some pretty good work.'

'Let's have a look at that machine,' I interjected. 'Can I switch it on?'

It was indeed quite a slow processor, running WINDOWS98. It 'felt' fine to me, I did a few quick hand checks and then plugged in my laptop for a more thorough investigation. All tests came up 'clean'.

'Seems OK,' I said. 'Can I do a bit of a trawl on the network?'

'Fine by me,' replied Alan, 'but I'm completely illiterate about these things. Just make sure you don't crash anything.'

'Don't worry, I ought to know what I'm doing.' As I was speaking, my laptop was sending out software agents around the Ethernet loops checking, interrogating. Everything looked fine, all the hardware seemed clean and I waited for the final message to appear that the checks had been completed. I waited. And waited. I pressed a key. Nothing. I pressed CONTROL C to interrupt. Nothing. The network had hung. Then a message appeared on the PC: 'CRAY going down.' That was it. Oh dear. How embarrassing. People were coming out of their offices and asking each other if their computer was working. The coffee machines would be much in use for the next twenty minutes.

It may not have been my fault. My software is pretty good, and not prone to causing problems. Perhaps it was a freak collision with some other specialist stuff, but it shouldn't happen. The network looked and felt clean. Maybe...

'Is there any way of finding out what else was running on the network?'

'No idea, I'm afraid,' replied Alan, 'but we'll go and have a word with Mike who runs computer support.'

'So its all your fault!' began Mike (bearded, of course) as we entered the machine room. But I could see he was smiling.

'I plead not guilty! What I'd really like to know is what else was running when the network crashed.'

'That could be embarrassing to some people. What they don't always realise is that we can watch every keystroke from here, so if someone's downloading porn from the Internet we soon know. Don't worry, I'll find out what went wrong, and if it's your fault I'll send you the bill!'

'I wouldn't do that if I were you,' I replied, 'I might just charge the department my company rates of £200 per hour!'

'Might as well adjourn for tea in the meantime,' said Alan. 'A good chance for you to meet the rest of the department!'

Half an hour later Mike had found something interesting.

'The CRAYs were very busy on some CPU intensive work at the time. Somebody was wasting the computer's time to draw Mandelbrots at very high resolution, millions of iterations per point or something like that, and for some reason this clashed with your software. I think it was just one of those flukes that occur when a system gets overloaded. No real harm done but I'll make sure that the unnamed person sticks to using his or her home computer in the future!'

I decided to forgo my travel expenses. I'd done nothing to help and only lost everyone half an hour's work. It wasn't till I drove away that I realised that I had, after all, been aware of something, something which I now noticed by its absence. Just a hint of something, connected perhaps in some way with the computers but not like anything I'd met before. I stopped and phoned back on my mobile. They'd let me know of any more developments. There seemed little else I could do.

Barely a week later and another phone-call from Durham. There had been another heart attack in the maths department.

It was Mike, the computer support manager.

He'd survived.

He was still in hospital and wanted to speak to me urgently. I dropped everything and hurtled over Stainmore on the A66 to be there in under an hour.

Mike seemed basically fine, he'd been fortunate in that he'd not been alone when he collapsed and his colleague had known basic resuscitation techniques. Propped up in his hospital bed, he began to tell me his story.

'Remember when we had the computer crash? I told you that someone had been playing at drawing Mandelbrots. It actually turned out to be some serious research to do with prime numbers, the same field in which John and Mary had been working. I'm not a mathematician myself but I vaguely understand the Mandelbrot set; every budding programmer cuts his or her first teeth on a Mandelbrot graphics package.'

'That's the fancy beetle with lots of attached buds and wavy lines? It didn't really appear till after my time in maths.'

'That's right,' said Mike, 'and every bud has a number associated with it, basically the number of times you have to repeat a simple equation to get back to the numbers you started with. Plot it on a computer and you get greater and greater complexity the more deeply you look. It's the classic fractal, the classic example of a simple process generating enormous detail.'

'So what's the connection with prime numbers?' I asked.

'As you probably know, prime numbers are of great importance in encryption and secure transmission of information; if there's a quick method of factorising numbers with hundreds of digits into primes, this could have enormous commercial as well as military potential. There's actually a simple connection between the Mandelbrot set and prime numbers. There is one main bud in the set. Smaller buds can be either round or, well, Mandelbrot shaped. Round buds corresponding to a prime number are ONLY found attached to the main bud. This fact isn't a lot of use in itself as it takes far longer to check a bud on the Mandelbrot than to factorise a number by hand. However Mary's team have done some clever maths and come up with what looks like a simple geometric test for primality using the Mandelbrot set, moreover if the number isn't prime, the hierarchy of buds immediately gives the factors. Mary was writing up the paper when she died. Or at least she had been. Apparently she found a mistake in the proof which left a loophole in the theory involving the number 37.'

'37 – why?'

'Don't ask me! Anyway it seems that she found this out after studying the notebook left by Michael Taylor...'

'You mean the ex ski-instructor who died in Austria?'

'The very same!'

Mike was getting excited. He looked tired and flushed.

'Look,' I said, 'I mustn't tire you out. Perhaps you should have a rest and I'll come back later.'

'Yes, you're probably right,' sighed Mike. 'A heart attack really takes it out of you. Why don't you come back at visiting time this evening.'

I came back at 6.30 to find screens around Mike's bed.

He'd taken a massive heart attack an hour earlier.

He was dead.

I phoned Alan Rendall and broke the news. I also told him that nobody must do any computer work of any kind until I'd been back...

If the maths department had previously been in a state of shock, now it was stunned. The press had also now discovered Norman Taylor's death. 'Fourth maths lecturer dies within a month.' Already conspiracy theories were being floated. The pressure was on.

The next morning, Alan Rendall introduced me to the young post-doc researcher, Tim Smith, who had been present when Mike, the computer manager, had collapsed. Tim was working in the field of prime numbers and Mandelbrots.

'Was Mike a Christian believer?' was my first question.

Tim was plainly embarrassed. Why some people react in such a way to the existence of God and the teachings of Jesus is one thing I've never understood. You might as well be embarrassed at the existence of the physical universe – or of prime numbers.

'I wouldn't call Mike a believer,' interjected Alan. 'He had an open mind but wouldn't have accepted a personal God.'

'Yourself?' I asked Tim

'Not really – no.' he replied, uncertainly.

'Right,' I said. 'Whatever we're dealing with is dangerous, evil. Whether you believe in it or not, unless you accept the help and power of the good God it will overwhelm you, as has happened to four people in the last month. What it is I mean to find out – now – before anyone else dies.'

'But we do maths, not theology here...surely maths is entirely neutral, whatever you believe,' countered Tim.

'That may or may not be so,' I replied, 'but I mean to find out. Could you please explain to me exactly what Mike was doing when he collapsed?'

'I needed some help from him in speeding up my methods. He was running one of my programs at the time.'

'That program – what does it do?'

'Oh it's basically a simple Mandelbrot routine, honed to pick out the buds appropriate to the numbers I'm studying. Professor Rendall probably told you that I was working with Mary in the field of prime factorisation of large numbers.'

'If I sit down at the computer, would you be able to take me through exactly what Mike was doing?'

'Yes, if you like but – er – is it safe?'

'It's safe for me. Liken me to the trained electricity linesman who can work on live overhead wires. But keep away yourself and do NOT look at the screen. Don't worry about me – I'll survive, even if it kills me!'

Tim groaned. 'I just can't get my mind round this. It sounds to me more like witch-doctoring than maths!'

'Call it what you like,' I said, 'just remember, four people have died.'

'OK' said Tim. 'Let me get the computer up and the software loaded.'

He switched the machine on, booted it up and logged onto the CRAY. A minute later the familiar Mandelbrot beetle appeared on the screen.

'Now,' he said, 'you can take over.'

'Remember,' I said, 'DO NOT look at the screen from now on. What does this program do?'

'We thought we'd got the prime number problem licked until we discovered a loophole for some numbers which contain 37 as a factor. That's no real problem in practice, a number comes out either as prime or divisible by 37. But it made the maths untidy, we wanted to understand why and if possible patch our method up. It occurred to me that we might get a clue if we could see what the sets actually looked like. The regions of the Mandelbrot that cause problems are really very small. You take the period three bud. Then take the subsidiary period three – that's period three multiplied by three, or nine. Then take the next subsidiary period two, then the subsidiary period 37 from that period two. This then has its own period three bud with its own period three, and so on. You know, the rhyme,

"Great fleas have little fleas upon their backs to bite 'em.

Little fleas have lesser fleas and so ad infinitum."

When you've done this process three times over you hit the first anomalous number. You need millions of iterations to display the set, hence the CRAY.'

By now he'd completely lost me. I'd just have to follow his directions.

'Were you running this program when the machine crashed a couple of weeks ago?'

'A very similar program, yes, as a matter of fact. No displays on that one, just doing various mathematical tests on the set. Mike thought I was playing games until I explained it was serious research. It was then that I got him involved to help me speed up the program – poor Mike!'

'Right, let's go...'

'Pull down the menu and click on "draw main subsidiary".'

I did as instructed.

'Enter "3" for the period three bud.'

Instantly the new, circular black bud with its wavy tendrils appeared.

'Now repeat the process. Enter 3. Now enter 2. Now enter 37.'

The Cray was so fast that the buds still appeared instantly on the screen, each one showing an ever increasing complexity of attached waving tendrils.

'We repeat the process twice more. That's when Mike collapsed.'

I alternately pulled down the menu and entered the numbers. 3. 3. 2. Then 37. And had a shock.

The CRAY cluster was now having to perform hundreds of thousands of iterations for each point and took a second or two to draw the picture. As it appeared I had that familiar sensation of skin crawling, of revulsion, something about that fantastically complicated network of tendrils just off the main bud.

'I think I'm onto something,' I said. 'Whatever you do, don't look at the screen.'

As I'd suspected, when I entered the next '3', things were worse. I'd enlarged the region that caused the discomfort. Then after the next '2', the picture enlarged to the subsidiary bud at the end of the period 3.

I remembered who I was. I remembered the good God. I remembered that the universe is made good, but still includes primordial chaos and evil.

I entered '37'.

Even with all the power of the CRAY cluster, the program was running slowly having to perform hundreds of millions of iterations at every point as the picture gradually built up on the screen. Which was as well. As each detail emerged it was like being hit by an electric shock. From the screen emanated pure, impersonal, naked evil. It would have killed anyone else. Which of course it already had done. I could hardly bear it myself but still watched in horrified fascination as every malignant and malevolent tendril appeared. Take the most beautiful scene you have ever seen. Invert it to ugliness and multiply it a million-fold. That was on the screen now.

'Getting anywhere?'

Tim's casual voice broke my reverie.

'Don't look,' I shouted, reaching with such haste for the 'screen off' button that my tensed muscles sent the monitor flying on to the floor.

There was a crash of breaking glass. Alan unplugged the machine.

'Are you OK?'

I must have looked white.

'Sorry. I'm good at smashing up computers. How about a cup of strong coffee.'

We sat in the tea area, as I slowly recovered. I knew now what had caused the deaths but was still baffled as to why, and what it meant.

'When that last picture started appearing, that was when Mike collapsed.' said Tim. 'Presumably the others were investigating the same area of the set.'

'I'm surprised it didn't kill him outright,' I said. 'Maybe he believed in God more than he let on... but what I don't understand is why that particular region of the set is so malicious.'

'Hang on,' said Tim, 'the Mandelbrot set is just an image of some basic mathematics. How can maths be malicious?'

'Who says maths is neutral? Proofs can be beautiful, can they not?'

'Yes, certainly. Indeed that's one reason why we were investigating. The beauty of Mary's proof was flawed by those particular period 666s.'

'Those WHAT?'

'You know, the period 666 buds. That's what you were looking at.'

'What on earth do you mean?'

'Simple,' said Tim.

'The first time round you looked at a 37 subsidiary of a 2 of a 3 of a 3. That's period $3 \times 3 \times 2 \times 37$ which equals 666. You then looked at the subsidiaries of that, or $666 \times 3 \times 3 \times 2 \times 37$, that's 666 squared. The third time round – when you broke our monitor – was 666 cubed.'

'And what would 666 to the power of 4 look like? I dread to think! Now I understand!'

Alan nodded. Now Tim looked puzzled. '666, what's special about that?'

'666. The Number of the Beast. The Book of Revelation, the last book in the Bible.'

'Hang on, how could something written thousands of years ago have any bearing on this?'

'That's a good question. The Book of Revelation was written when Christians were undergoing the most appalling persecution and torture. The second part of the book was written in a kind of code so that only the initiated could understand it. A terrible beast comes up out of the sea bearing the number 666. The best explanation for the number 666 is that it codes for the Latin version of the name NERO, the mad Roman Emperor who had unleashed the terrible persecutions. The writer of Revelation was forecasting the return of Antichrist, the incarnation of all evil, in the form of Nero. But the number crops up elsewhere, too. For example. Take a simple code where $A=100$, $B=101$, $C=102$ and so on. Then $H=107$, $I=108$, $T = 119$, $L= 111$, $E = 104$, $R=117$. Add them up, and HITLER $= 666$. Coincidence?'

'Wait a minute, you could make almost anything total 666 if you tried hard enough!'

'Maybe. But now we have evidence that there's something very basic and evil connected with the number 666. Something built into the very fabric of the universe, into the very logic which underpins its laws and regularities. Perhaps it's no coincidence that the names of two of the most evil people the world has ever known are related to that number.'

'But what can you do about it?' asked Alan.

I laughed. 'I'm not God! I can't change the laws of logic! When God made this world he made it good, but he made it out of chaos and that primeval chaos still surfaces from time to time. Danger is everywhere! Geologists after all, have to be wary of volcanoes. Biochemists have to treat viruses with great respect. Chemists have to learn how to safely handle acids and explosives. Now we know that even pure mathematics can be dangerous; you'll have to write a code of practice for investigating period 666 Mandelbrots just as the chemists do for working with hydrofluoric acid...'

Tim shook his head. 'I still can't understand how a simple iterative mathematical process can harm anyone.'

'No doubt psychologists will explain it by some resonance between the complex patterns seen by the eye and the circuitry of the brain; undoubtedly the devastating effect of those images will have some such explanation on that level. Scientists naively believe that, when all the laws of nature are uncovered, they will be beautiful. It's their religion. Christians know better. The world is good, but evil is still powerful, a force we now know is present even in pure mathematics...'

Program restarted

It was end of term. The corridors and rooms which had so recently been full of young people, which had throbbed with loud music for half the night and been filled with the smell of coffee for half the day, were quiet and empty. Bins were overflowing, stuffed with the posters and pictures which had adorned walls until only a few days before.

Only a few lonely postgraduates were left, awaiting the fresh influx of Summer conference visitors. In the computing department the network was at last quiet, the gateways no longer overloaded with student Internet surfers, the processors no longer desperately trying to cope with five hundred fledgling programmers. Now the system managers could take things a bit easier, could spend time deleting passwords, erasing files and removing all the timebombs and amateur viruses that jokers had deposited in the system when they left. There might even be a bit of time for some real work.

The department seemed very quiet without the throng of students working all hours of the night trying to finish their projects. No queues, physical or telephone, at the help desk. A few research students were still working on long-term projects but most of them kept office hours, so, for the first time in weeks, Tim had the whole department to himself on the evening shift.

A couple of the new PCs had been constantly crashing. Tim suspected a virus and reckoned that now was as good a time as any to sort the problem out. He was just about to about to boot the first one up when a young lady with curly blonde hair whom he'd never seen before walked into the room.

'Can I help you?' asked Tim in that sort of voice which really means, 'What are you doing here, who are you, how did you get in, and I'm busy.'

'The security man said that I'd find somebody here who might be able to help,' said the girl in a vaguely American accent.

'Did he,' said Tim.

Tony on security was a nice bloke, but he mustn't let just anybody charm their way in. He should have phoned me up first, thought Tim. Have to have words with Tony...

'Actually I'm rather busy at the moment, perhaps you'd like to come back during working hours tomorrow and put your enquiry to the help desk?'

'No. That'll be too late. I need help now.' She spoke with a note of urgency, even panic. Tony groaned inwardly. He hadn't any real excuse for not helping, it was only that he'd been looking forward to a quiet evening sorting out some long delayed problems. Perhaps it would just take five minutes.

'OK,' he said wearily, 'what's your problem?'

'I was told that you had some old computer equipment here. I've got a box of cards I need read in...'

'CARDS!' exclaimed Tony in amazement, 'what part of the Stone Age do you come from?'

'Look,' said the girl, 'never mind that. Can you help?'

'Well, perhaps, I suppose. I was setting up something of a museum here. We've got an old card-reader and an IBM 20-50 workstation from the early seventies, just for demonstration purposes. I'm not sure I could link it to a modern network though.'

'Doesn't matter,' said the girl, 'as long as you've got something that will run FORTRAN4.'

'FORTRAN WHAT? We've got FORTRAN99 on the network but I doubt if its as back compatible as THAT. When was FORTRAN4 – before transistors or something?'

The girl didn't seem to appreciate the sarcasm. 'I'm told it was a 1960s code. Look, I was told there'd be no problem with FORTRAN4 on punched cards.'

'Who on earth told you that! I wasn't even born when we stopped using punched cards here!'

'Look, I'm sorry. I never thought a few years would make such a difference – I mean your computers are still electronic aren't they?'

She asked the question with such innocence that Tim wondered for a second if she really meant it.

'Well, I can only give it a try. But I can't promise anything.'

They went out into the corridor and along to an unmarked door which Tim unlocked. Inside was a jumble of ancient equipment: card punch machines, teletypes, paper-tape streamers, tape-drives...

'Here we are,' said Tim, wheeling out a dusty card-reader attached to a large old computer box with keys along the front. 'You actually had to boot this machine up by hand, feeding the initial instructions into memory using these keys. It would then read in these cards – he pointed to a handful already in the reader – which set the machine up. It used to connect to a teletype but now we link the machine to a standard PC for demonstration purposes. We had it going only a few weeks ago for the "History of Computing" module, so you might be in luck!'

He wheeled the old workstation down the corridor into the main computer room and plugged it into a multiway socket. Another lead connected the machine into the back of a PC. Tim sat down at the keyboard.

'What's your identifier?'

'Identifier?' said the girl in her innocent American accent, 'I don't think I've got one!'

'Well what do you want me to do with the data on these cards if I read them in? Haven't you got some space on the network?'

'Space on the network – I don't quite understand.'

Tim sighed. 'If you want to read data in and run a program

you must be a registered user with your own password and file-space. We obviously can't allow anyone access to the system.'

'Look. Please, all I need is to run the program. I don't need anything else.'

'But you've got to store your output somewhere – I mean do you know anything about computers?'

'Look, I was told that you just used line-printers for output.'

'I don't know who told you all this but it sounds like they haven't seen a computer for 30 years!'

'Please,' said the girl – she sounded near to tears and didn't look as if she was putting it on, 'could you please just help! All I need is a line-printer output!'

Probably a deadline for some arts project, thought Tim. No idea of computers at all and I expect her supervisor hasn't been near the things since he was a student. Oh well, I'd better see what I can do.

'The only thing we still use a line-printer for nowadays is payroll,' said Tim, 'but if I change the paper it should do.'

He went to a cupboard and pulled out a big cardboard box. 'This hasn't been used for years; I'll throw away the top few sheets,' pulling out the dust-covered top layers, tearing them off and crumpling them into the bin, 'and feed the rest into the printer.'

He opened the top of the printer, released the payroll paper and replaced it with the leading sheets of the old continuous-feed paper. 'Centre it, and set top of form,' – the printer whirred briefly – 'and we're ready to go. I'll use my own file space,' Tim continued, sitting down again at the PC. 'What's your name?'

'Does it matter?'

'Well,' replied Tim, a little surprised, 'I just wanted a name to give to the file.'

'Call me Zim.'

Time shrugged his shoulders and set up a sub-directory called 'Zim'.

'Right, let's try and read these cards in.'

Tim switched on the old work-station; a row of red lights

appeared above the switches. 'I actually have to key in the starting binary addresses by hand.' He toggled the eight switches, pressed a button, and repeated the process a few times. Red lights flickered on and off. Suddenly the card reader sprung into life, the bootstrap cards disappeared into the machine and emerged in the output tray. A message appeared on the PC screen:

'2050 ready'.

'Now,' said Tim, 'I've set up a file to read these cards into a file called "Zim.dat". When we've done that we can try running your program.'

'I don't think that will work,' said Zim (was that really her name?), 'the program has to run straight from the cards.'

'Same thing,' said Tim, 'we just copy the cards onto a file and then run the program from there. Have you got those cards?'

The box was half full and Tim was surprised to see that the cards were made of plastic.

'Not seen any like that before,' he commented, before feeding them into the reader and typing 'read' into the PC.

The card-reader whirred for a second or two and stopped. A message appeared on the screen: 'Program restarted'.

'Blast!' said Tim. 'Have to reboot the workstation and try again.'

He removed the plastic cards and fed the bootstrap cards through again.

The second time round the same thing happened, after a few of the plastic cards had been read, the message 'Program restarted' appeared.

'Look,' said Zim, 'I didn't think it would work. Try running the program as you read in the cards!'

'I suppose I could set up a pipe straight to the compiler,' suggested Tim, 'but I'd be surprised if it works. I'll use our old FORTRAN77 compiler, if that doesn't accept the coding there's nothing I can do.'

Tim rebooted the workstation again and set up a few software links on the PC. This time, after a few cards had been read, the workstation stopped but didn't crash – and then began, slowly, to read in more. The PC screen stayed dead.

Suddenly the workstation picked up speed, cards hurtling through. The PC screen started flashing, then displayed a few lines of Greek and special characters. The last card disappeared through the reader. The PC screen went blank.

'Doesn't look hopeful, nothing happening, I'll try and...' began Tim.

' No, wait,' interrupted Zim, 'it'll take a minute or two to run.'

Two minutes later the printer suddenly screeched into action. Paper was going through faster than normal, just a few characters on each page.

Almost simultaneously a phone rang. Tim picked it up.

'Hello, Durham University computing department.'

'This is Oxford,' came the voice over the phone, 'we've just lost our network. It seems to have been taken over by a virus. It looks like it came from Durham, could you check your system please?'

Tim immediately tried the adjacent PC.

It didn't respond.

He tried an interrupt. Nothing happened.

'Our machines aren't responding either, I'll investigate.'

'You'd better shut your system down. Were getting reports in now from all over the place. The virus seems to be spreading across the Internet!' Tim put the phone down.

'Got a problem, I'm afraid. Have to shut the system down.'

'NO!' said Zim, 'It's working!'

The printer suddenly picked up speed, spewing out paper at pages per second. Each page was covered in characters and symbols, a completely meaningless jumble, yet Zim was staring intently at the printer window as if reading the pages flying past beneath.

Ignoring her, Tim went to the main server console and pressed the emergency reboot button. Nothing at all happened. He pressed the emergency shutdown switch. Nothing happened.

'What's going on!' he shouted across the room.

'It takes all the computer power available, it's using every machine on the Internet now, just a few more seconds...'

Horrified, Tim went for the main power switch as the printer accelerated into a crescendo scream, far faster than it had any right to work. But before he reached the switch all the PC's in the room simultaneously beeped. The printer stopped and Tim noticed a strong smell of burning. The phone rang. Zim was nowhere to be seen. Feeling like an overloaded processor himself, Tim picked up the receiver.

'The Internet has crashed. Sounds like every linked computer in the world has fallen over. We suggest you disconnect your system and reboot.'

Tim replaced the phone. All was quiet, totally silent, not even the hum of disc drives. The printer was smoking gently, Tim hurriedly pulled out the gently crisping paper – and felt the hairs rise on the back of his neck. On the last page was a portrait, in dots and stars, of Zim, with an obviously male figure beside her. Her hand was raised as if in farewell, below the picture were the words 'look – thanks'. Beyond, skilfully drawn in line-printer symbols, was an impossible range of fractal mountains and behind, three moons hanging in the sky.

In a daze he wandered across to reboot the PC network. On the screen of each machine was the single message: 'Program restarted'.

GPS

The rising wind howled down the black November corrie as we sat round the fire in the Ghorm-Coire bothy. Violent squalls of rain and hail rattled and roared on the roof. The weather was getting worse but the fire was blazing, piled bog-pine roots steamed as they dried and the bothy kettle was singing above the flames as we prepared another brew of hot, sweet, smoky tea. A row of wet socks, also steaming nicely, hung on a string above the fireplace whilst dimly visible in the flickering fire- and candle-light were several rucsacs, pairs of boots and other sundry items of gear scattered around next to the crumbling white plaster of the bothy walls.

I sat on a great lump of pine root, too big for the fire and too much of a challenge for a blunt bothy saw. Jane and Steve occupied the two bothy chairs which had been carried in years ago after being thrown out by some Highland primary school.

We'd all had a hard day in the hills, the couple bagging remote 'Munro' (3000-foot) mountain tops on the plateau while I'd packed in from Elphin across miles of peat-bog and swollen river. This was the best part of the day, relaxing by the fire while the storm rose outside.

'We really found the GPS system useful on the tops today,' said Steve. 'Takes all the sweat out of navigation! Not only does it tell you where you are, you just have to punch in the grid reference of where you want to get to, and it shows you not only the direction to walk but also tells you when you're there!'

'GPS – that's "Global Positioning System" isn't it?' I asked.

'Yes,' replied Steve, 'uses communication to an array of satellites to provide a precise fix on position and direction.'

'But,' I continued, 'what if the battery fails, or you punch the wrong grid reference? I think I'd rather stick with the good old map and compass!'

'And what if you're in an area of magnetic variation, or you set your compass wrong from the map?' replied Jane. 'Also the compass only gives you direction, not distance. There's much less scope for error with the GPS system – and that means it's much safer.'

'I'm not sure that I agree,' I countered. 'Yes, you have to be experienced with map and compass before you venture into difficult country. But once you know how to use them they're pretty infallible. You soon get the knack of judging distance. Reliance on technological gadgetry in the hills is dangerous.'

'A compass would have been considered a technological gadget once upon a time,' said Steve, 'the thing about technology is that it allows you to cross the hills safely in conditions when otherwise it wouldn't be possible. Even such simple things as modern waterproofs.'

'OK I accept that,' I said, 'but there's no substitute for experience. If you rely on GPS to lead you over the plateau like a dog leading a blind man then I'm sure you'll come a cropper sooner or later...'

It was just a bit of good-natured banter among experienced hill-goers around the bothy fire.

The storm had blown out by the morning; there were still a few light rain showers but the wind had dropped and the weather seemed to be improving. The forecast had suggested a weak ridge of high pressure and it looked like the forecast might be right. I set off on the long walk to Bonar Bridge; first over the mountain behind the bothy then about 20 miles down the glens. Steve and Jane planned to spend a couple more days in the hills completing this particular group of Munros.

I'd been home several days before I heard on the Scottish news that a couple was missing in the mountains near Bonar Bridge. I phoned the police and discovered, as I'd feared, that it was the pair I'd met at Ghorm-Choire. I told them what I'd known of their plans and suggested that they might have stayed an extra night or two at one of the bothies. The weather had deteriorated again and the mountains were being lashed by heavy rain on mild south-westerly gales. In such conditions even small streams become impassable obstacles and travel in the Scottish Highlands, away from the roads, can be virtually impossible.

A week later and Jane and Steve were found. Dead. They'd been staying at Glen Dearg bothy and had written in the log-book that they'd be doing a circuit of hills including Ben Dearg. The weather was poor with low cloud and rain, but not particularly severe for experienced hill-walkers. They appeared to have fallen down crags above Loch Tuath. Reports mentioned that they were well equipped and even carrying a GPS navigation system...

Glen Dearg was one of my bothies. For many years I'd been a member of the organisation which looked after these remote shelters and I had particular responsibility for this one, my job being to check up on it from time to time and to organise repairs as need be. I resolved to go out there and have a look at the next opportunity.

Just a week later, and there was another hill tragedy in the same area. A lone climber had fallen off Seana Bhraigh, one of the remotest hills in Scotland. Although well equipped with ice axe, crampons and GPS system he appeared to have walked over a cornice in poor visibility.

Then another party went missing in bad weather having set out from Glen Dearg to climb a couple of lower Munros adjacent to Ben Dearg. Conditions had been reasonable initially, just low cloud and light snow, but the weather had deteriorated, first into a full blizzard with a storm force wind from the south-east and then into heavy sleet and rain.

Two men and a woman were eventually found, having died

of exhaustion and hypothermia after a severe battering by the weather. They were miles off course, near Glen Docherty. Again they were well equipped. I made enquiries and, yes, they were using a GPS system. It was conjectured that, in the severe conditions, they had chosen to walk with the wind at their backs rather than descend in the correct direction but with gusts of up to 150mph on the plateau even this had proved almost impossible. A spokesman for one of the mountain rescue teams involved in the search commented that over-reliance on modern technology could have been partly to blame for all three tragedies. He also mentioned, interestingly, that he had sometimes found GPS systems unreliable in the Ben Dearg area.

In early March I set out for a weekend at Glen Dearg bothy. I live in the Far North and it only involved a few hours by train then a ten mile walk through the glens, not usually difficult even in bad weather. There had been a lot of snow on the mountains but a thaw was now in progress with wet avalanches falling off crags, and rivers running high. The last river before the bothy can be impassable when in spate so I chose a route over high ground, crossing the streams near their sources.

It was a real slog. The cloud was down and the wind was sheeting drizzle and rain across the bleak snow-streaked landscape. Once above 2000 feet there were fields of deep, wet snow, I wallowed waist-deep through snow-filled peathags and struggled across fast-flowing streams flanked by high banks of wet snow. I wasn't worried though, there was all day, I was well equipped with map, compass, food and waterproofs and just looked forward to the bothy fire, a good meal and a night's sleep. Conditions at 3000 feet were pretty appalling, but the wind was from behind and I simply plodded on, quite enjoying the violence of the elements. It was a case of taking careful compass bearings, following the left-hand ridge, keeping west and north of the main tributaries of that river.

Just below the 2000 foot contour, on a particularly bleak col of peathags and slush, the cloud blew temporarily clear to give views down a side valley to two lochans, fading out into the driving drizzle. That was where the bodies of Jane and Steve had been found, below those crags where the recent avalanche debris was now piled.

The last couple of miles was really tough, a wallow through peat hags and porridgey slush and a slippery descent of a hillside streaming with water. The bothy didn't seem quite its usual friendly self when, soaked and pretty tired, I eventually reached it. The river was in full spate – I'd never have crossed it – while the main valley was completely flooded. It looked as if I might be there for a couple of days as getting back home in those conditions could prove tricky. Fortunately I'd come prepared with plenty of food.

At first I thought that the bothy must be occupied. There was quite a lot of gear in the main room, sleeping bags, stoves, food. I glanced in the book and saw that the last entry had been made by that party of three who'd set out to do a couple of Munros and never returned.

The first thing to do was to change into dry clothes. Next, light the fire, there wasn't a lot of wood in the bothy but I'd collect more from the bogs when the weather improved. Then to light a couple of candles and put a pan of water on the fire to boil for tea. I gathered the scattered gear and piled it all together in the corner of the other room, somebody would have to come out to collect it when the weather was better. At last I could sit down by the fire, enjoy a mug of smoky bothy tea and start writing about my epic crossing in the bothy log-book.

Needless to say I wasn't expecting anyone else to arrive in such conditions, so I was very surprised when I heard the outside door open. There was a bit of clattering and banging before the door shut and the inner door was opened. I was still more surprised to see it was a youngish lady, swathed in waterproofs, clutching a bicycle front light and a couple of panniers.

'You timed that well,' I said, 'tea's just brewed!'

'Oh, I could just do with a cup,' she said, 'hang on a minute, I'll just go next door and get changed.' She emerged about five minutes later, an attractive blond in perhaps her late thirties.

'Where have you come from?' I asked, 'I wasn't expecting anyone else in tonight.'

'Took the bike over from Inverlael,' she replied, 'carrying on through to Inverness tomorrow.'

It always happens. You think you've had a pretty tough day and managed rather well, really – and then find somebody else has done twice as much and thinks nothing of it.

'Wasn't it pretty hard going with a bike?'

'It wasn't too bad. I came over the tops to avoid the rivers, even managed a bit of cycling down through the snowfields. Yourself?'

I confessed that I'd just ambled across from Black Bridge.

'Could be a bit tricky getting out tomorrow if the weather continues like this,' I continued.

'Well I've got to be back in Inverness tomorrow night so if the river's too high to cross I'll probably take the route you came in today.'

'I found it... quite hard going, even without a bike.' I said, 'There's still a lot of deep wet snow about.'

'Don't worry,' she replied, 'I'll survive, even if it kills me!' and then laughed. 'That's my motto. But, seriously, I've seen much worse. I'll make an early start. Who else is staying?'

I explained about the recent tragedy. 'It's odd,' I said, 'there have been three fatal accidents in these hills in the last few months and all seem to be linked to over-reliance on GPS navigation systems. You're not using one yourself are you?'

'No way!' she laughed. 'I'm a specialist computer investigator, so I don't trust any computer-based system!'

'I must say, I don't trust them either,' I replied. 'Nothing like the good old map and compass.... you know I was saying the same thing to the couple in Ghorm-Choire last November who very sadly came to grief near here.'

'By the way,' she said, 'I'm Lynne. And you?' 'Norman.'

We spent the next hour or so cooking our meals. I was pleased to see that Lynne, too, used the old-fashioned but reliable Primus stove.

I volunteered to venture out into the storm to do the washing up, leaving Lynne looking at the bothy log book. It was still lashing with rain and very mild, with the river roaring down the mountainside accompanied by the rumble of dislodged boulders. I glanced at her bike when I came back in, I'd expected a sturdy modern mountain model but no, it was an old-fashioned lady's sit-up-and-beg with three-speed Sturmey Archer gears, complete with basket attached to the handlebars. She, like me, was obviously not one to follow the modern fashions.

'I like your bike!' I said.

'Oh, just the thing for dragging across mountains. Tough as anything, and the basket's ideal for map, compass, food – just where you need it...'

She hesitated a moment. 'Have you looked at the recent log-book entries?'

I hadn't, yet.

'All three are from those people you were talking about who were killed. Look.'

There was an entry from Jane and Steve. They were setting off for Ben Dearg. The next entry was from the Ullapool Mountain rescue team, collecting the couple's personal effects. Then there was an entry from a Bolton man who'd gone off to climb Seana Bhraigh. A couple of weeks later – friends, collecting his gear. Then there was the entry of the three people whose gear was still in the bothy.

'And I come here to get away from such things...' she said. 'You say they all had GPS systems?'

'Yes – they do have a reputation for being unreliable around here.'

'I wonder why that is,' Lynne replied, in a tone of voice that suggested she knew something. 'Changing the subject – any stories about this bothy?'

As a matter of fact, there were. It is entirely true that the last couple to live in the bothy, in the nineteen-thirties, met a tragic end. The lady, who was shortly expecting a first child, had drowned, probably as a result of losing her balance when the river was in spate. The husband was making his way up the valley and found her body floating in a slack pool. He committed suicide by hanging himself from the bothy door. The bothy has since had a reputation for being haunted, not that I believe in such things myself.

People hear scratching and scraping noises. Doors rattle and open themselves. There are thumps upstairs, dogs refuse to go into the bothy, that sort of thing. Well I've heard bats scraping and mice scratching, many a time. The wind eddies in strange ways and sudden gusts even on a calm night can rattle the door, or throw it open if it's not properly fastened. Dogs will crouch, snarling at a beetle or at a bat hanging on the wall, which humans may not notice. Having fastened many slates on the roof myself I can vouch for the fact that they will rattle or thump in a gale. Stags will roar outside or even scratch their antlers on the bothy walls. In short there is an entirely natural explanation for everything anyone has heard or seen. I'd spent many a night alone in the bothy and it had always seemed a friendly enough place.

'I thought as much,' said Lynne. 'Poor people. And now we've had three more tragedies. They won't be meaning any harm, it's just that modern technology confuses them.'

Now it was me that was totally confused. It had been a hard day. But there were more surprises in store.

'I'll just confirm my suspicions,' said Lynne, disappearing with torch into the other room. She returned with a small leather case which opened to reveal a very swish palm-top computer. It didn't quite fit with the candle-light and a woman who brings an ancient bike and cooks on a Primus stove. 'Always take this with me, just in case.' She switched the machine on; within seconds the desk-top display was glowing, obviously a pretty powerful model. She typed a few commands, manoeuvred the pointer, clicked, watched the display for a few minutes then switched off.

'As I thought,' she said, 'just sad, confused spirits. Nothing evil. I'll be able to help them and make sure we don't get any more GPS problems.'

'What IS going on?' I asked.

'Sorry,' she replied, 'to me this is just work. Those two sad spirits have been around here for years, they've never even met mains electricity, or television, and they somehow get tangled up with the computer navigation systems and send the electronics haywire. It's about time they found peace. In their day, suicide was a terrible sin and their branch of the church was not over-strong on forgiveness. With hindsight I can see that I was called here specially.'

We've all heard the phrase 'being at a complete loss for words' but for the first time in my life I knew what it meant. I was completely speechless. I've met some weird bothy people but this was ridiculous.

As if reading my thoughts Lynne went on.

'You don't have to believe any of this if you don't want to. Just put me down as another bothy weirdo. But there will be no more GPS problems, no more hauntings. Don't worry though if you hear a few funny noises tonight.'

I didn't hear a thing. Exhausted, I slept solidly and soundly in a way I rarely do at home. I was up early, I thought, but found the bothy empty. Lynne had gone. It was still raining, the rivers were an incredible sight, full spate, as high as they ever get. She must have headed up over the hills, bike, computer and all. Or had I dreamt the whole thing? She'd left no entry in the book. There was no sign of her presence, though there were a few chalk marks on the floor of the other room which I probably just hadn't noticed the previous night. I packed up and girded my loins for a hard crossing of the hills back to Black Bridge.

It was another epic wallow through bogs and slush, even the smallest streams were major obstacles, everything that ever ran with water was running with water. I never saw any bicycle tracks or even footprints but Lynne might just have taken a different route. I could barely imagine what it would be like to drag a bike across those hills in such conditions... you meet your match, sometimes. Or had I been dreaming?

There were indeed no more GPS-related accidents in the area.

It must just have been an unfortunate coincidence. But a couple of months later I did receive through the post, a business card: 'L. J. Thomas. Specialist Computer Investigator'. The address was South Stainmore, Cumbria. On the back was a little handwritten note: 'Dear Norman, please let me know of any more problems, see you again sometime perhaps? Love, Lynne'.

The fastest bathroom
in the universe

A blue-white column opened over the house, like a cosmic lift shaft disappearing up into the Monday morning rain-cloud. The bin-man, who'd just attached the wheely-bin to the lorry and was watching it tip, disposable nappies and all, saw the bright light out of the corner of his eye.

'What the...'

A red, saucer-like object rose, then disappeared up the blue shaft at impossible speed. The cloud glowed red, briefly. The light vanished.

'Bloody Hell – what was that! They'll never believe me at the depot...'

The Chief Executive held, between two tentacles, a sealed glass phial containing about half a litre of colourless liquid.

The top executive suite was the apex of many thousands of square miles of chemical and processing plant situated just inside the perpetual dark zone of the rocky planet. This, the highest spire, projected three miles above the surface into permanent penumbral sunlight from the hottest blue-white star in the cluster and looked across, through darkened shielded glass, to the dazzling glow of the bright side of the planet. There, solar collectors, covering half the globe, powered the manufacturing processes at the headquarters of Intergalactic Pharmaceuticals and produced antimatter to drive the interstellar delivery flights.

'This quantity of elixir is worth more than an entire solar system. As you know, just a few billionths of a gram provides eternal youth as well as being an irresistible aphrodisiac for the vast majority of inhabitants of our local cluster of galaxies. Yet it's only a waste product for the beings which produce it!'

An elite group of top management, beings of all cultures and configurations from half a dozen galaxies, had been assembled at a cost of only slightly less than the phial of elixir. All, in their own sensory ways, were assimilating the chief executive's message and eagerly awaiting the reason for their summons to headquarters.

'We have tried to obtain permission to establish a colony of the creatures, from which the elixir is harvested, in our home star cluster. However inter-galactic law deems this a violation of the rights of a native culture. The good name of the company prohibits illegal abduction, though, as you know, other less scrupulous organisations, have resorted to that route.'

'We are now about to attempt, with full government permission, an improved harvesting technique. It is at the limits of technology. Only our ownership of this star cluster gives us the enormous quantities of energy required. Only our huge corporate wealth has allowed us to develop the fastest starship in the universe, has given us access to the latest inertial damping and space-time splicing techniques, has enabled us to attract the most highly trained and expert pilot. It will allow us make the round trip across the galaxy in approximately ten minutes.'

'Respectfully, sir,' interjected a company chief accountant, 'that's only twice as fast as we can manage now – that will give at most a five-fold improvement in product quantity.'

'May I respectfully remind you that accountants don't run this company! If I may continue. We can make the round trip of some 200,000 light years in ten minutes, using full power anti-matter overdrive together with maximum reverse time-travel. With the latest space-time splicing techniques combined with massive inertial damping, it is now feasible to adopt the totally revolutionary approach of...'

Jay, who'd heard it all before, drifted off into his own thoughts. It was only the opportunity to pilot the starship that had brought him to this artificial office three miles out into space on the dark and depressing side of a dead planet when he'd rather be basking in the glorious radiation from the blue-white star. He'd normally take at least a leisurely three or four weeks for a trip across the galaxy under his own power, stopping off on the way to linger in the plasma and particle streams of some well-loved neutron stars. Yet if he had a weakness it was for speed. Only a plasma-vortex being like Jay had the ability, the intimate knowledge of the galaxy, and the nanosecond reaction time to make such a journey possible. Only a being for whom organic products and money had no influence or attraction could be trusted by Intergalactic Pharmaceuticals on such a mission.

The Chief Executive was still speaking. 'After almost a year's full output of our entire anti-matter plant,' he gestured, with a sweep of a tentacle, across the whole of that amazing view from the window, 'we now have the energy requirements for our first mission using the new technology. What is even more important, we've finally had the go-ahead from the galactic authorities. We have the craft. We have the pilot. Welcome to a new era in Intergalactic Pharmaceuticals!'

The three day outward journey across the galaxy was very routine for a being like Jay. There was no hurry, no product on board to degrade, every incentive to conserve energy. Computer control was entirely adequate and Jay didn't even bother to check the instruments until the craft was in orbit round a dead moon in the destination planetary system.

It was indeed a bleak spot in the outer fringes of the galaxy, a remote location which had saved the system from exploitation and destruction in the eras before galactic law. A few very ordinary planets orbited a small yellow-white star with nothing else nearby, a long long way from anything that mattered. Yet in this unlikely spot lived the primitive civilisation which produced the most coveted product in the universe.

Margaret locked the door with great relief; a few minutes in the bathroom was the only time of the day she had to herself. With her pair of toddlers happily watching the Teletubbies there was a real chance that she mightn't be bothered. What a life, when the only time you could get peace was when sitting on the toilet! As her bowels began their natural processes she thought of her friends, just home from sailing round the Hebrides with a new-born baby and two toddlers. Then there was Michelle who managed three children as well as a full time job and had just spent two weeks climbing in the Alps. How did some people do it? The furthest she managed to get was to the shops, and that took most of a morning to plan. Oh, for some real travel...

'Can't understand anyone wanting to live in such a desolate star system,' thought Jay, 'but never mind, work to do.' First, a quick nip into the asteroid belt to gather matter for the return journey. The inertial fields drew a 20km diameter chunk of icy rock into the fuel tank, where a small nugget of quark matter collapsed it to an ultra-dense state. The other fuel tank already held a trillion tons of anti-matter. At least there was no fuel tax out here!

The facts are known to almost every sentient organic life-form throughout the local cluster of galaxies, except of course to those primitive enough not to have developed interstellar travel. That most sought-after and costly brew of complex compounds, that elixir of life, that fountain of eternal sexuality and youth over which devastating intergalactic war has more than once been waged, is found solely in the waste-products of females of the species known to themselves as 'human'. It has defied all attempts at synthesis. To the life-forms concerned, incredibly, it is of no value and thrown away in vast quantities, contained within what is derogatively known as 'shit'. The highest yield comes from the waste products of young adults who have recently given birth to and fed young, and for various complex reasons is found in especially high concentrations in particular genetic lines.

Because the product degrades very rapidly after it has left the body it is essential that processing be carried out as soon as possible. Collection and shipment to the manufacturing plants has never been managed in less than ten minutes, by which time only one part in 10,000 of the original quantity remains. Illegal abduction of females has frequently been attempted but the criminals concerned never have sufficient resources to make more than a fleeting success of this route.

Now an entirely new approach was being attempted...

The bathroom door had not yet closed before Jay's craft was hovering, invisibly, by the house. As the bolt clicked shut, atomic splicing fields sprung out, slicing through the house. Molecular positions were recorded, a hologram generated.

In just a millisecond, a small anti-gravity field with minimal inertial damping sent the craft, with bathroom firmly attached, out into space. Now for the bit Jay had been looking forward to. He did the plasma-vortex equivalent of a human pressing the pedal under his right foot to the floor. With antimatter drive and inertial damping set on maximum, Margaret, sitting on the toilet and thinking longingly of travel, rocketed at unimaginable acceleration towards the centre of the galaxy.

Within 30 seconds the craft had reached top speed having converted a trillion tons of matter and antimatter into pure energy and ejected a rocket beam of ultra-high energy particles. The craft was now travelling so fast that it would have lost a race across the galaxy against a beam of light by just two centimetres; this combined with maximum reverse time-travel gave an effective speed of 300 light years per second. Margaret was travelling faster than any organic life-form had ever travelled in the entire history of the universe.

To a human, the inside of the craft would indeed have looked remarkably like that of a fast car. A computer generated display, which the driver faced, replaced the windscreen. There was an accelerator and a brake, also a steering wheel and two fuel gauges, one for matter and one for anti-matter. Jay was driving fast, and enjoying it. The computers deviated the craft around dark stars and other small objects; the bathroom now had enough energy to disintegrate a planet like a light-bulb struck by a bullet. All Jay had to do was to control the main sweep through the galactic centre and out across the spiral arms to the far headquarters of Intergalactic Pharmaceuticals.

A human observer would however have been completely overwhelmed by the computer display, stars hurtling from nowhere to fill the screen in a blue-white glare then vanishing within fractions of a second. Ahead was a huge dust cloud, the apex like a hand with three great fingers each a light-year long. The craft hurtled through the gap between two of the outstretched digits, close to a new, hot blue star whose intense radiation was evaporating the dust and uncovering stars just lighting up as dusty globules now tenuously attached to the main cloud. Creation in action. How ever much he travelled, Jay was always impressed by the sight.

At the centre of every galaxy lies a super-massive black hole, with its attendant inward-spiralling bands of matter. From the poles, beams of radiation jet out at immense energies. By skimming close to the edge of the black hole, the so called event horizon, and then riding out on the polar particle beams, Jay could gather even more energy.

Should you stray inadvertently beyond the event horizon of a black hole, no energy or technology in the universe can rescue you from being dragged ever inwards till ripped apart by tidal forces and swallowed into nothing but mass, charge and angular momentum. So Jay was concentrating hard in the milliseconds up to that close approach. This was all very familiar territory to him, many a time he'd surfed out into space on the particle beams or bathed in the radiation from the nearby super-massive star which was one of the brightest in the galaxy.

Yet the star had gone! In its place was an expanding sphere of brilliantly glowing debris. Jay had just missed one of the most spectacular events in the galaxy, the catastrophic supernova explosion of one of its brightest stars. He stared, hardly believing what he was seeing.

Alarms were ringing. He'd been distracted for a crucial microsecond. The inertial damping was being overloaded. Too close! He wrenched the steering wheel and just in time veered from within a few kilometres of the event horizon of the black hole. Ultra-relativistic plasma and intense radiation almost overwhelmed the craft's fields, Jay felt the tug of immense forces, the inertial damping was concentrating on shielding the vulnerable organic passenger. He dived the craft into the safety of the outgoing particle beam...

Margaret, sitting on the toilet, felt something like a brief wave of dizziness pass over her. An odd feeling, nothing quite like she'd felt before, it seemed almost as if she and the room had been turned inside out. She must be suffering from stress, or was she coming down with a bug? What she needed was a holiday – how she envied those who could take off and see some of the great sights of the world!

Just outside the force field was one of the most amazing views in the galaxy, one only ever seen by the plasma-vortex beings or the rare organic life-form wealthy enough to afford the immense amounts of energy needed to travel safely in such an environment.

Two large stars, one a huge distorted red ball, the other a blinding blue-white, were being drawn inwards as they orbited close to the central black hole. Gas ripped off their outer layers formed a glowing disc, shining in all colours from red through white to intense blue. Meanwhile, larger in-falling clumps of gas, not to mention the occasional hapless planet heated to nuclear fusion temperatures, exploded in soundless brilliant bursts of energy. Further out, a huge torus of dust fluoresced yellow and green in the X- and gamma-radiation emitted from the central power source.

From each of the poles of the black hole an intense radiation beam bored out into space from the greatest particle accelerator in the galaxy, punching clean through the obscuring dust to be detectable down the line-of-sight to galaxies billions of light years distant. So energetic was the beam that by riding down it, Jay was able to yet further boost the speed of his already ultra-relativistic craft.

Within seconds the black hole was in the far distance and Jay could relax, swinging the craft up through the spiral arms of the galaxy to lock onto the deceleration beam from the Intergalactic Pharmaceuticals star cluster. By driving the craft straight into a focused beam containing the entire energy output of a hot, massive star, Jay and his precious cargo would be brought to a halt within 30 seconds. Computers locked the craft onto the precise point in space, the matter-antimatter field generators sprung into life to provide the required shielding, the inertial dampers wound up to full power...

Ultra high energy particles sprayed out in all directions, a few to eventually collide with the atmosphere of some distant inhabited planet and cause intense speculation as to the origin of such impossibly energetic cosmic rays. Sitting on the toilet, in the middle of the highest energies since the creation of the universe, Margaret felt, and saw, absolutely nothing. The inertial damping fields had been designed to cope with this. Her bowels were emptying themselves nicely now, she had always been very regular.

The landing was routine. Like a red-white angel from space the craft dropped out of nowhere into the midst of the vast arena of lights covering the dark side of the planet which formed the manufacturing centre of Intergalactic Pharmaceuticals. Instantly, glowing tubes sprung out and fastened onto the odd, box-shaped object attached to the sleek craft.

Margaret could hear her toddlers singing along happily with the Teletubbies. (Speaking across the galaxies with Top Technology from Tachyon Telecom!)

She flushed the toilet.

'Perfect timing!' The water, and its priceless contents, were whisked in micro-seconds to the main processing plant. A few milliseconds later and the elixir had been separated from those ingredients which degrade it, while already Margaret was back in space.

'We've done it! The yield is incredible, it's millions of times greater than we've ever achieved before and exceptional quality. Now its just up to Jay to get that life-form back to its own planet without breaking any rules...'

Meanwhile Jay had filled up his fuel tanks with the trillion tons of quark matter/anti-matter required to slow down, fast, on the other side of the galaxy. The focused energy beam from the hot star accelerated him rapidly up to full speed and the 300 second journey back across the galaxy began.

All was well.

Margaret wiped herself the usual three times and flushed the toilet again.

It had been decided to sacrifice the trace wipings even though, had they been collected and speedily processed, the product could have been sold for enough to purchase a small planet.

She filled the wash-basin, wiped her lower regions with a sponge, rinsed it out and emptied the basin. She filled the basin again and began to wash her hands.

The ritual was precisely the same, every time.

Jay was giving the galactic centre a wider berth this time, hurtling through an area of dense globular clusters, huge spherical jewels of blue and red, each point of light a star, one of the wealthier parts of the galaxy. About ten-thousand light-years from the destination, he began to prepare for landing and braked, hard. The matter/antimatter propulsion fired, full power in reverse, enough energy to make a quiet central main-sequence star go nova. More intense particle beams pulsed out across the universe and the craft swooped in past the sun and plummeted through the atmosphere of Earth. Within milliseconds the bathroom was back in place, the field generators switched off.

Two seconds later Margaret clicked the bolt and opened the door. Had she been in there just ten minutes? Her legs felt a little wobbly. Must take things a bit easier, she thought. Need a holiday!

'Made it,' thought Jay, 'now lets get back and have a look at that supernova!'

Not even plasma-vortex beings, however, are immune to the occasional mistake. He'd relaxed, his mission was over. He accidentally turned off the invisibility field with the tachyon transmitter, just before boosting into space...

Sermon software

The meeting had been, as usual, churchy. The annual Anglo-Scottish gathering in London – affairs academic, and heights above, or below, the earthy practical concerns of a parish minister. Why did he come? Perhaps it just did him good to be jerked out of any complacency by the blatant worship of the gods of sex and money in the capital. That talk on computers had been worth listening to though; maybe it really was time to drag his church into the 21st century.

With plenty of time before his train north, the Rev. David Marsden chose to walk, through the crowds and roar of London. People were so interesting to watch, especially when for once nobody knew him. Everyone was hurrying, head down, looking only at his or her own square of pavement.

Dusk was falling over the long Charing Cross Road. The roads were solid with headlights, sometimes stationary, sometimes accelerating forward like a burst dam from changing traffic lights. Somewhere, above the noise and lights was the sky, and the weather, as on another planet.

As jewellers line the square of St Mark in Venice, so computer and hi-fi shops line the lower Tottenham Court Road. Here you can purchase anything from a second-hand vintage 486 to the latest gigahertz MAC. 'Computer purchase is a jungle, not to be entered without a good guide and plenty of expert advice', so had said the speaker at David's conference. It was thus only out of curiosity that David looked in the occasional window, he certainly wasn't going to contemplate any purchase without first consulting the Church of Scotland computer adviser! Here was a shop window covered in posters. 'Unrepeatable bargain. Bankrupt stock. Complete computer system with free software. One tenth of normal retail price, only £100'.

Somewhat to his surprise, David found himself opening the door into a rather scrappy shop with piles of boxes, a counter half covered in computer screens and a salesman in shirtsleeves. As always his dog-collar commanded immediate attention.

'Yes sir. We're being completely honest about this offer. It hasn't come off the back of a lorry. Small company somewhere up Burnley way – Pendell Computers – did their own thing and produced a system completely incompatible with anyone else's. Not surprisingly they went bust. The receiver wants it cleared as quickly as possible. All good stuff if you just want a standalone system and we're offering a two-year guarantee on the hardware. Twin floppy, printer, monitor. Can't guarantee the software though, not at this price!'

David tried to look knowledgeable.

'Hmm, sounds good value, all I really want it for is writing, and perhaps a bit of filing.'

'Yes, writing. That's what Pendell were specialising in. You get a whole box of writers' software, good stuff I'm told, but you can always just use the floppies as blanks – would cost you £30 just to buy the clean discs!'

David had only just learnt about computers but had gathered that floppy discs were a little dated.

'Doesn't everyone use CD-ROMs these days?' he asked, trying to sound as if he knew about such things.

'Yes, to some extent that's true,' replied the salesman, 'but if you only want the machine for personal use you've got everything you need here, a few years ago this would have been a top range system worth £5000!'

David was not an impulsive man.

'Suppose I think about it for a couple of days and then phone you, would you be able to send it me then?'

The salesman knew exactly what kind of man he was dealing with.

'They'll all have gone I'm afraid, selling like hot cakes. We've only got these left and we've sold 43 today already.' He waved his arm over 20 or 30 boxes.

David spent the rest of the journey home wondering if he really should have written that cheque and somehow the Almighty didn't seem to be passing him messages either way. Meanwhile the salesman was delighted at another mug willing to pay good money for an out-dated and redundant computer system that didn't even have a CD reader, but then what could you expect for only £100?

Three days later a delivery van called at the manse near the small border town of Baubles and unloaded a huge cardboard box. David, who lived alone, had just been on his way to visit Mrs McPherson and her varicose veins – and decided that she could wait another day. Inside, among lots of packing, were more boxes bearing mysterious inscriptions. It was a bit like his childhood Christmas! Soon he had all the components out, and connected together as the salesman had shown him. He switched on, there was a BEEP and the screen showed a friendly question mark at the top left-hand corner. David typed 'HELLO'.

'ILLEGAL COMMAND' came back the unfriendly reply. David sighed. He'd have to read the beginners' manual.

More than one kindly old body missed the usual visit from the minister that week. 'Poor man, living all alone. Must be ill, probably not looking after himself properly, needs a good wife he does!' They said it to him every week, so they said it to each other instead.

Beginners' manuals are never written for beginners. David, however, was not a man to give up easily and after three days had discovered how to use the word-processor, if in a very simple-minded fashion, and how to save his work on a floppy disc. To use the printer was harder and he'd had to phone the London shop to find out how to stop it printing everything on top of itself on one line. The correct command to change things was on page 178 towards the end of Appendix E and referred to the advanced manual (not included with the computer) for more details.

Saturday came and the Sunday sermon was still unwritten. Usually David would take a day off on Thursday, hill-walking, communing with God, and by the end of the day the outlines of his Sunday service and sermon would be well in place. A busy day of visiting would follow on Friday with Boys Brigade in the evening and more visiting till late. Saturday morning was spent doing the week's shopping, when he wasn't talking with members of his flock whom he met in the street.

On Saturday afternoon David would take the phone off the hook, lock the door and settle down in his study with Bible, commentaries and notes for a couple of hours of hard but rewarding work on the material which his subconscious had been processing for most of the week. It was, other than for his day off on the hills, virtually his only time of undisturbed quiet.

On this week most of Thursday had been spent trying to get the printer to print. He'd made a rushed visit on Friday to Mr Young who'd just gone into hospital with terminal cancer, but had otherwise spent his time working out how to insert and delete text and how to carry out back-ups of his discs. Saturday morning, after a quick round of the supermarket buying tins, was spent attempting to write a BASIC program to add two numbers. He decided not to bother with programming for the time being.

This Saturday afternoon when David sat down in his study all he could think of was floppy discs and printers and text editing. As far as sermons went his mind was a complete blank. It was, I suppose, a temptation that came upon him. 'I've got three clear hours. Maybe now is the time to have a look at some of that free software! I'll just have to use my reserve sermon.'

Five minutes later he was eagerly sitting in front of the computer screen inserting the first Pendell floppy disk:

'Writers' software – index and introduction'

BEEP and an outline of a hill with a steep scarp slope appeared on the screen with 'PENDELL COMPUTERS' written across it. 'WRITER's PACKAGE. DOUBLE CLICK TO CONTINUE.' David knew how to double-click but it had taken him an hour to find out. Feeling like a real expert he clicked the mouse twice.

There was a series of BEEPS and a page like the index of a book appeared on the screen. Each chapter was on a separate disc or set of discs.

1. INTRODUCTION
2. MILLS AND BOONS
3. SPY STORIES
4. SCIENCE FICTION
5. WESTERNS
6. SEX
7. MODERN NOVEL
8. MODERN PLAY
9. MODERN POETRY
10. GENERAL POETRY
11. THE JOURNALIST
12. THE TRAVEL WRITER
13. THE SERMON WRITER
14.

David didn't see what 14 was. Resisting a sudden urge to load disc 6 and without bothering to see what was on the rest of the first disc he turned to disc 13 – or, rather to his surprise, a dozen discs all in one separate box marked: 'The Sermon Writer'.

He loaded the first disc.

'Welcome to Pendell Computers' most famous and important product, the unique Pendell sermon writer. Our discs hold the entire text of the Bible in the New International Version as well as all the major commentaries. There is a complete library of ten thousand famous sermons. With our famous interactive sermon writer, Saturday afternoon blues are a thing of the past! Surprise and amaze your congregation by your new power and strength! Your church will grow as never before...', and so on it went, in similar vein. 'Hmm. Not surprising they went bankrupt with hype like that!' said David to himself, inwardly congratulating himself that he wasn't the sort of person to be taken in by that kind of thing. Yet it was with eagerness he clicked the mouse to display the first 'menu.'

A set of numbered options was intriguingly displayed.

1. Automatic sermon generation
2. Assisted sermon generation
3. Sermon library
4. Concordance – the WORD processor
5. Old Testament
6. New Testament

Not particularly liking the look of options 1 and 2 he clicked on number 3, 'Sermon library. Please load disc 3.' David took disc 3 and put it into the disc drive. But something was wrong. When he tried to get the disc catalogue all that came up was the message: 'Broken directory'. Too bad. Well he didn't really need a sermon library, he had shelves of sermons already. He tried item 4, and the same thing happened. And 5, and 6. The Bible, the famous sermons and the concordance were simply not there or at any rate were inaccessible to him. The salesman had said, after all, that the software wasn't guaranteed.

'Doesn't look much use this, might as well see if 1 and 2 are working,' thought David, and clicked on option 2.

PLEASE LOAD DISC 2A prompted the machine.

David loaded disc 2A. There was a peel of electronic beeps, obviously trying to emulate church bells.

'Please state main theme of sermon or ask for suggestions' said the screen.

David typed, 'Jesus'.

Back came a long list of suggestions: Birth, Death, Resurrection, Miracles, Healing, Son of God and so on. David clicked on 'Miracles'. Immediately another long menu appeared on the screen: general, healing, nature, water/wine, withered hand, fig-tree, walking-on-water, feeding 5000...

David was enjoying this, and wondering how far the trail

would lead. He clicked on 'walking-on-water'. Now a question appeared on the screen: 'Please give desired length of sermon, in minutes.' A believer in giving his flock value for money, David typed in '25'.

Another menu appeared on the screen. 'In 25 minutes you can choose to put over between one and five main points. The recommended number is three. Please choose main points from the following:'

This time the list embodied just about everything anyone had ever said in a sermon on the subject, from 'eschatalogical significance' to 'mastery over nature' to 'Jesus is always near' to some decidedly baffling phrases such as 'Was Peter right?'

David chose the recommended three main points and, since he had himself, as he thought, preached everything possible on the subject, decided to see what some of the more baffling phrases meant. He chose: 'The seashore', 'The shortcut' and 'Was Peter right?'

Back came another question: 'Please select denomination' and from a list which included Greek Orthodox and Mormon he chose 'Church of Scotland – Low.' Next came a couple of questions on the average age of the congregation and the location of the church. The final question was perhaps the most important:

'Select type of sermon from the following:-'
and the list read:-
1. Right wing fundamentalist
2. Evangelical
3. Middle-of-the road liberal
4. Radical
5. Social gospel
6. Death of God

David, naturally, selected the third option.
It is a characteristic of any complex computer program that it ALWAYS contains 'bugs'. The errors which prevent programs running have usually been found and corrected, but there is always some combination of options, perhaps never before tried, that leads to something unexpected happening, something the

programmer never intended. Usually the program just fails without giving any clear indication as to why. The more subtle errors which lead to wrong answers or incorrect results are harder to find...

Any computer expert would simply have said that there was a bug in the program – after all, the programming outfit had gone bust and the software had never been fully tested. It was perhaps strange though that the error occurred at this most crucial stage, five o'clock on a Saturday afternoon and no sermon prepared for the morrow. Needless to say, instead of providing option three the computer, loaded option six : 'Death of God'...

At first nothing happened. Then the message appeared 'Generating sermon. Please wait.' (David could hardly believe his eyes). Just 30 seconds later the message appeared 'Sermon completed. Do you want to print it?' David clicked on 'OK' and the machine replied 'sermon printing.' Unfortunately nothing happened. David had forgotten to switch on the printer and by the time he had, the sermon was lost.

He had to go through the whole procedure again. This second time, an incomprehensible gibberish of letters and numbers came out. Something was wrong. There was nothing for it but to search the 'sermon writer' manual. After another half an hour he had located the section on printer control in Appendix E, this time on page 182.

Two hours and three strong cups of coffee later, having fiddled with almost every possible printer setting he finally got the sermon to print... HORROR it was 7.30, he had to be at the youth club in half an hour and hadn't yet had anything to eat.

By the time the youth club was over and he'd spent an extra hour and three quarters with a hard case who was gradually softening up, it was far too late to think about sermons. There would still be time in the morning.

David was just finishing his Sunday morning breakfast when there was a knock on the door. It was the local doctor, an energetic lady in her fifties. 'She's just died on me!'

She looked, David thought, more angry than upset. Nevertheless, consolation was clearly in order.

'Come in, come in, sit down.'

It then transpired, to the minister's relief, that it was the doctor's car that had failed right outside the manse, on the way to an urgent call seven miles up the valley.

David had to take her in his own smart car to the isolated farm, half a mile down a muddy track and then wait while the doctor ministered to a child with severe earache. Back at the manse there was barely time to change, collect Bible, order of service and sermon and set off for church on the other side of town, in a car which now looked as if it belonged to a farmer. David had intended to take his 'spare' sermon, kept in reserve for emergencies such as this and he could never understand how it came about, when he stood up to speak, that he found himself with a computer print-out in front of him...

A preacher of David's experience was quite capable of putting up a good extempore performance. The Holy Spirit would have given him the words in his moment of crisis. But perhaps it was lack of faith, perhaps temptation, maybe something else, for some reason, when the words of the machine-produced sermon which he had not even looked at were in front of him, he began to read them out aloud.

Immediately David realised that it was powerful stuff. The words seemed to have a force of their own, and his voice acquired new strength and majesty, booming from the pulpit as it had rarely done before.

Everyone was alert, looking, listening, taking it in, even old George who would usually by now be dropping off to let out loud snores when David reached the key part of the message.

'It is now accepted by all the main theologians that Jesus never, in fact, walked on the water. The Greek was mistranslated; Jesus was, in fact, walking on the seashore. The myth gained ground in the second and third centuries and some of the gospel accounts, such as that of Matthew, were doctored to give it more credence.'

David, of course, knew about the translation ambiguity but had never come across such a firm resolution of it. He found himself listening intently to his own sermon. He heard that Jesus had simply been taking a shortcut across the sands at the end of the lake and had, in fact, been trying to avoid his disciples so as to go into hiding for a few weeks. His mission was failing and he was considering a change in direction. Peter had run after Jesus and persuaded him, reluctantly, to rejoin the company.

'This is one of the frequent instances where the Biblical accounts are most misleading and must be interpreted with a great deal of care. The argument is indeed strong that the Bible should only be read by trained experts. What the story here actually tells is of one of the ways by which Jesus was led astray and persuaded Into the wrong path, the path that ultimately led to the disaster of the cross.'

As his concluding words rung round the church David felt he had never preached a better sermon. The obviously intense listening of the entire congregation was clear confirmation. The rest of the service passed in a sort of self-congratulatory daze. People were strangely quiet as they left the church and David too was thinking about the new revelations of his sermon. A whole new way of looking at things was opening up.

During the week he seemed to have fewer callers than usual and his visits were also over more quickly. There was more time to get the hang of his new computer system and in particular that marvellous sermon writer. He tried a few out, the ideas were so fresh, new. He wondered how he'd missed the obvious himself. He read a sermon on prayer and learnt that conscious, verbal prayer was of no use as God already knew everything. God had never meant people to waste time praying when there was so much to be done in His world! He learnt that God made the world to be enjoyed. He learnt that 'sin' was an invention of the Pharisees, subsequently taken up by a Puritanical church, the rot beginning to set in with the misunderstandings of Paul.

He decided to preach the sermon on prayer as of immediate practical use to his flock. Saturday came – and no sermon to write! He could lie in bed all morning and potter round the shops in the afternoon.

The church seemed a bit emptier than usual on Sunday. Obviously too much doom and gloom around, people not enjoying themselves, getting low, catching colds and flus. He preached his sermon on prayer and enjoyed it – and decided to eat out in a local hotel for a change instead of cooking his usual roast.

The next week was quieter still. He could lie in during the mornings, take his time over life for a change. Thursday came, but he didn't really feel like his usual hill walk. 'Not been the usual pressure. Don't need it.' Instead he lay in, got up about 11, wandered down to town for a bar lunch and then stayed in the bar till closing time. It was definitely more healthy to enjoy company than to wander over bleak wet hills on his own.

Come Saturday night and what better than a bottle of whisky by the fireside. The church really had got it wrong about 'sin', he decided.

Sin made a good subject for his sermon the next morning. Eleven o'clock was far too early for a service, he now realised. No wonder there weren't many people along! Still, splitting headache or no, he had to go, it was a good thing his printer gave such clear typing or with his double vision he'd never have been able to read the sermon. Even with a somewhat slurred speech the words still took off on their own and echoed superbly round the three-quarters empty church.

The winter had been remarkably mild, with virtually no frost and snow. It was nearly the end of March, almost four months after the famous sermon on Walking on the Water, when the weather changed. A vicious blizzard drove down from the north, such as the area hadn't seen in years. When David struggled out of his bed at about noon on Saturday the manse was dark and cold and the windows caked with drifted snow. He went to switch the light on and cursed; the power was off.

David had given up lighting fires in the last month or two – too much like hard work – and instead would burn electricity.

There was nothing for it now though. He opened the door to find a near white-out of gale-blown spindrift. It took ten minutes to get to the coalhouse and return with a bucket of coal, by which time he was cold, miserable and out of breath from the unaccustomed exertion. But there was something about the wild weather out there, something seemed to be nagging at his mind.

Eventually the living room fire was going. He put a pan of water on the flames and, when it boiled, made a cup of tea. He sat back drinking the delicious if smoky tea, the fire warming him as the blizzard howled outside, enjoying a simple pleasure in way he had not known for a long time.

Then a sudden, piercing thought. He had to prepare his service and write his sermon and with no electricity he couldn't use his computer! Then, like a reply, another thought – why bother. Nobody will be at church tomorrow anyway in weather like this. Just sit back here by the fire and doze. Nobody will expect you to get out.

But the service wouldn't go away. He'd never missed except when very ill. He must try. His study was cold, and dark. 'You'll never manage without the computer. You've got out of the way.' So went his thoughts, like a voice in his head.

David had been a resolute man, and the last four months had not yet got rid of all his resolution. Once he'd decided to do a thing he would do it. He decided to get that service prepared and that sermon written.

The study door was locked. David realised he hadn't been in for four months and couldn't remember where the key was. It was no good searching the house in the growing dusk of a wild afternoon with no electricity. Better just go back and enjoy the fireside – and there was a nice half-bottle to finish... But no. Without realising that this was a crucial point of decision in his life, David decided he'd just have to get that sermon prepared. He went to his tool box for a hammer and an axe and in two minutes of surprisingly enjoyable vandalism had the door open.

The room felt odd, cold and lifeless, the friendly desk lamp not working, the windows plastered in snow. He collected his notebooks and a concordance, dusty from lack of use. But where was a Bible? Then he remembered getting a pile of heavy books to stand the computer terminal on...

The computer occupied pride of place in the back room but looked strangely dead. Yes, the terminal stood on a pile of books; he searched through them but still couldn't find a Bible. Wait a minute, perhaps his Bibles had gone into the loft with the computer boxes.

The step-ladder to the loft was in the shed. Again came that temptation to give up the idea, to enjoy a quiet half-bottle by the fire, cosy with the storm raging outside. It was only his old stubbornness that made him don coat and wellies and venture out again.

The blizzard was, if anything worse. The shed door flew open in the wind and nearly came off its hinges. The steps folded up and trapped one of David's fingers, breaking the nail. He tripped over and fell headlong in the snow trying to carry them across the garden in the gale and then went and put them through the glass in the porch.

With frozen fingers he erected the steps and climbed up to the hatch into the loft, torch in hand. Just as he was scrambling through out went the torch. The bulb had failed. Still, he knew where the boxes were, just to the right of the hatch. He felt with his hand – CRACK! David yelled with pain and issued most of those words which he'd never used until recently. A mousetrap had caught his sore finger.

Yet the boxes were there. He dragged them down the steps and inside, covered in dust and plaster, were all his Bibles.

Back in the living room it was nearly dark and the fire had gone out. David was no longer surprised to find that he was out of firelighters and that he'd knocked his only box of matches into a pool of melted snow. There was only one thing left to do. Putting on all his warm clothes, taking Bible, notebook and concordance he went out to the garage, got into the car and turned on the interior light.

Dust shook off the covers as David opened the Book. And his eyes immediately fell on the passage:

'Be still and come out of him!'

He flicked over the pages again and read,

'Something like scales fell from his eyes.'

For the first time in three months David found himself praying. And, until the car battery failed, at about midnight, he read the Bible as if he had never read it before.

The snow had turned to horrible wet slush by morning but the power was still off just outside the town, where the manse stood, and the roads were blocked. David set off on foot an hour early so as to get to the church in time.

Come eleven o'clock and he walked down the aisle. But where was everyone? Five old ladies, pillars of the church since 1945, sat in the back row. There was one other person under seventy, indeed under forty, Lorna, the doctor's daughter, sitting alone in the middle row, looking miserable. There was nobody else except the organist, who had been coming to the church since he was baptised in 1931.

Must be the weather, he thought. Well, it would make his penitential sermon bit easier.

It was the hardest sermon he'd ever preached. The words no longer came out of his mouth on their own, he had to force each one out and it then seemed to drop like lead into the cold and empty building.

'I come to you Lord, not worthy to look up, like the tax collector and sinner. I ask forgiveness from you, and from you my congregation...'

Never had the hymns been so thin, never had the service seemed so long and difficult. But at last it was over. He stood at the door as everyone went out. The old people shook hands politely as ever, they had outlasted several ministers and were quite prepared to sit it out till this one went. But it was Lorna who cheered him up.

'Great to see you're better! That was a tremendous sermon. You must come for lunch, it'll be a bit bleak out there with no power!'

As David tucked into a good Sunday lunch with Lorna he realised what a stupid hermit-like existence he'd been leading over the previous few months. He told Lorna the tale of the computer.

'Too much living alone, that's your trouble, never mind computers! What you need is a good wife to look after you!'

David had heard this sentiment almost every day since he took up the call at Baubles and was quite used to politely ignoring it. Yet, for the first time, it occurred to him that perhaps it mightn't be such a bad idea after all...

The snowplough had been through by afternoon and Lorna ran him home. He asked her round for tea the following Saturday.

'Now mind that computer of yours!' was her parting remark.

The electricity was back on and the first thing David did was go into the back room where the computer was. Odd that he'd never noticed before, there was something peculiar, even unsettling about the layout of screen and keyboard. Something wasn't quite straight, or the proportions were out, or something. He felt a strange reluctance to sit down at the keyboard. But now he knew who was in charge. He was a minister of the Lord. Powers of evil there might be but the powers of good were stronger.

Resisting a feeling of sudden revulsion he powered up and loaded the first disc. The friendly beeps came up but somehow sounded more like a hideous cackle of laughter. The Pendell logo of a hill with a steep scarp slope came on the screen. The logo also showed a large bird flying just below the crest. He'd never looked at it closely, always being in too much of a hurry to get on to the sermon-writer proper, indeed he couldn't actually remember having noticed it before. He looked more closely, curious to see whether it was a buzzard or eagle, or just some graphic designer's sketch.

It was a witch on a broomstick.

His growing suspicions had become certainty. He typed into the keyboard, 'In the name of the Father, the Son and the Holy Ghost I command you to come out!' and pressed the carriage return button. Nothing very dramatic happened. Just a soft pop and the screen went blank. A thin wisp of smoke started curling out of the back of the computer. David hurriedly switched it off. Five minutes later the computer, disc drives and screen were safely in pieces in the dustbin.

He lit the fire and threw the discs on, just to be on the safe side. As the last of the sermon software went up in flames it seemed to him that he heard a hellish scream, fading away into the cheerful roar of the fire and that the room was suddenly brighter. But perhaps that was his imagination.

The secret glen

It's over 20 years since I discovered the strange valley of Dirc Mhor. I'd been trekking across the Scottish Highlands for a couple of weeks, lightweight tent on my back, crossing empty mountains and moors, descending every few days to some remote village shop to restock supplies. The fortnight had started with the usual days of rain and mist but the weather had changed unexpectedly into a glorious settled spell with day after day of clear views and unbroken sunshine.

It had turned fine enough for the rare delight of mountain-top camping and the previous night had been spent at 3500 feet. In the evening I'd ambled around the edge of the plateau, watching the shadows grow in the glens as the sun dipped down to the west. I'd only one day of the trip left before returning to the stresses and problems of 'normal' life.

Whilst many hillwalkers aim for the high 'Corbett' and 'Munro' tops I enjoy exploring lower, less-frequented country and planned a last long day's trek across rolling moorland hills which didn't even quite make the 2000 foot mark. After another night out I'd head down to the Great Glen for the long journey home by bus and train.

Dirc Mhor was only a name on my map, marked as a gully or little craggy valley cut diagonally across a gently sloping hillside. Since it was only slightly off my direct route I thought I'd take a look at it.

The moors had indeed been grand, miles of vast open skyscapes with the golden-plovers calling; a feeling of complete peace, a place where nobody other than the gamekeeper or the deer-stalker ever set foot. There were peathags and bogs, but there were also bare stony ridge-crests with short heather and mountain thyme and pink moss campion. There were little streams singing down shallow moorland valleys, there were the tiny nests of willow-warblers in the tussocky grass.

The features of the next high ridge, only two miles across the valley, had melted into a growing heat-haze as I started descending an ordinary rough moorland slope of patchy long heather and wet tussocky grass, with some bare peat, the odd boulder and a sharper edge just ahead. Then the ground suddenly fell away in front of me.

A huge cleft, looking thousands of feet deep in the haze, lay below. It was as if some giant had taken a great scoop to the mountainside, a U-shaped gash interrupting the gently falling slopes of my hill which continued, at the same angle, half a mile away on the other side of the canyon. Almost vertical slopes levelled out below, I could see a relatively flat valley floor with heather and peat-hags, some grass, a stream meandering through. The whole feature was about a mile long, opening out into the main valley and with a vertical headwall cut into the mountain about half a mile to my left. Especially interesting was a long narrow loch in a little cleft lying towards the valley head; this wasn't marked on my map and looked a fascinating spot to visit.

The air was utterly still, bees buzzed on the heather, a few flies circled. Nothing else moved in the afternoon sun, the valley basked in the heat as if asleep.

I hadn't the time – or more realistically, the energy, to have a better look. There were many miles yet to walk before camping that night. I followed the edge of the strange valley for a few hundred yards then reluctantly turned away, back onto the moorland ridge. Someday I'd be back.

I could find little mention of the place in the literature. Lying miles from any road and in the middle of country of little interest to most walkers, it would be rarely visited. In the past though, before the Highland clearances, such a spot would have been well known and must have had many stories and legends attached to it. What a place to hide an army, or even a band of robbers! Even these days the local gamekeeper would know every square inch of the valley, where the fox dens were, where the eagles and peregrines nested, the deer sanctuaries... quite probably estate guests went fishing in the wee loch.

The 'someday I'd be back' lengthened into over 20 years. In spite of many treks across the Highlands and Islands it was always the places I'd never explored that beckoned, there were Munros, and Corbetts...yet I often thought of Dirc Mhor. It was on impulse, at the end of October, that I decided to spend a weekend exploring the area. The red deer stag stalking season was over, but the rut would still be taking place and there is nothing more evocative than the Highlands when the stags are roaring their challenges to each other across the russet hillsides. Often the weather can be wild in an exhilarating sort of way, with force ten gales and rain then sudden gleams of sun on tops white with the first snow.

The journey by train and bus took the best part of a day and it was late afternoon as I tramped up the estate road in gentle rain to the keeper's house. It's as well to seek advice and permission in late Autumn as the keeper is still culling the deer hinds and you can be very unpopular if you scatter the animals from the area where he expects to find them.

It was the usual arrangement, a big Victorian lodge house set on a bluff in the trees with views out over the glen, the keeper's cottage a few hundred yards away with barns, stables and kennels. The dogs had already announced my presence and the keeper, a short but very fit-looking man in his early fifties, came to the door. I could see into the room behind him, a kettle was steaming on a kitchen range with wet clothes hanging to dry.

I asked if it would be OK to cross the hills and camp out for a couple of nights.

'That'll be fine,' he said, 'I'm not planning on starting the hind cull for another week or two. Like to give things a rest after the stags. Where were you thinking of going?'

I mentioned Dirc Mhor.

His face fell. 'No, I'm sorry, I can't let you go up there at this time of year. It's our deer sanctuary.'

I'd heard this kind of thing many times. Usually it's just an excuse for keeping you out. I tried again.

'It's OK,' I said, 'I know all about deer. I'm a bit of an amateur photographer, like to stalk them myself and get some good photos. I won't disturb them at all, they won't know I'm there!'

'Sorry,' said the keeper. 'There's no way I can let you go up into Dirc Mhor at this time of year.'

'When would be suitable?' I asked.

'I don't know what you'd be wanting to go up there for,' replied the keeper. 'Queer sort of place. Certainly not for a lady to go on her own, I'd say.'

When I first started hillwalking it was almost unheard of for a (then young) lady to walk the mountains alone. Even in these days of sexual equality I don't meet many other lone women on the hills. Unfortunately some of the older generation still haven't quite got used to the fact that women can be just as fit and tough as men in the mountains.

'I'd just like to have a look at the loch, see what lives in the glen – it must be a great place for wildlife.'

'There's nothing there,' replied the keeper. 'Just heather. Besides, it's private land.'

By now I could see I was getting nowhere. The initial friendly attitude had gone. I shrugged my shoulders. 'Oh well if you don't reckon it's worth a visit – the rest of the estate's OK?'

'Fine by me, as long as you keep away from the hills around Dirc Mhor. You won't see much in this weather, though.'

'It's all right for you,' I replied, 'living here all the time! Some of us just enjoy the peace and quiet of the hills, whatever the weather!'

And on that more friendly note we parted. I trudged on up the track into the late afternoon rain.

It was good to be back in the hills. The river was high and brown, foaming down over rapids to the left of the track and overhung by golden Autumn birches and rowans scarlet with berries. The track emerged into open hill country beyond a small pine plantation. Wet slopes of grass and heather with patches of dying bracken rose into the mist and streams cascaded downwards. It had obviously been wet for a while, but it wasn't cold. The keeper would likely check up on me so I took the branch of the glen that led away from Dirc Mhor; I'd descend into the valley and camp near the loch the following evening. Now I'd just carry on into the deep hills as the dusk came on and put the tent up in the gloaming. From time to time I could hear that marvellous sound of the stags in rut, baying challenges to each other across the glen.

There's no night's sleep like the first night in a tent in the hills, tired out after a long day of travelling and walking. The roar of the hill burn and the patter of rain on the tent soon lulled me to sleep, only the baying of the occasional nearby stag rousing me briefly.

The rain cleared overnight to one of those glorious bright Autumn days, sun and a bracing wind, clear air and long views over yellow and brown hills. I tramped a wide circuit of ridges, enjoying the uncluttered freedom of the moors, to approach Dirc Mhor from the far side. I was sure that the keeper would have gone up there on such a good day so I planned, late on, to descend unobtrusively into the far end of the glen and camp near the long, narrow loch. There was no way I could be doing any harm at this time of year and couldn't understand his concern. Maybe he was worried about the spawning salmon but it was more likely that the estate owner had simply instructed him to keep people out.

Keeping off the skyline I carefully approached the edge of the steep slopes falling into that strange valley. It was certainly an impressive, unusual spot. I lay down and got my little spyglass out; was that white dot a vehicle just past the far end of the valley? It was indeed a Landrover. The man would surely though soon be heading back for his tea, it was after five and the sun would be setting in another hour and a half. After another 20 minutes I saw the white dot move, the Landrover was heading back down the main glen. As soon as the vehicle was out of sight I started picking my way down the steep slopes towards that dark loch 1000 feet below.

It felt more like September in the now calm and warm air as I descended into the shade of the valley. Already I could spy a good camp-site on a green sward just upstream from the narrow loch. I might even manage a dip, there's nothing like the freedom of swimming in the nude in some remote Highland loch!

A stag, high on the left-hand hillside, with a harem of perhaps 20 hinds was roaring in response to a challenger about a quarter of a mile away. The air was thick with the Autumn scent of dead bracken and heather. As I reached the valley floor the temperature dropped suddenly, the cold air was pooling, there could well be a frost that night. The loch would be quite warm though, after the day's sun, and the thought of a swim to wash off the sweat and peat of the long trek grew more appealing. First I put the tent up on an ideal grassy spot by the young river. The water level was still quite high, but falling, and I had no worries about being flooded out now the weather looked more settled. Then I set off down to the loch.

The river tumbled over a 30-foot waterfall into a little tree-lined gorge which widened out into the long, narrow loch between steep slopes. A small rowan, still bearing a few red berries, grew out of the rocks to the left, overhanging the water where the deer couldn't reach it. The water was very calm. I stripped off (there was nobody for miles to see!) and waded in from a little sandy beach near where the river ran in. The water was cold but not too cold, I like to go in slowly and only started swimming when the water reached my chest. Fantastic! Swimming gently across the quiet loch under the pale blue sky – the peace... a large 'plop' nearby surprised me, the salmon must be rising, or perhaps a large trout!

Then, without warning, something BIG grabbed my legs and pulled me under.

There was no pain, no teeth – but something had tight hold of me, I couldn't kick, I was going to drown... I reached down and grabbed, it was something soft. I'm no good at holding my breath underwater, already my lungs were gasping for air. I punched, grappled. Something like a nose? I grabbed with one hand and squeezed, pulled and scratched as hard as I could with the other.

Suddenly the grip lessened. I kicked, hard. I was free.

Only an Olympic swimmer would have beaten me back to the shore.

The loch was calm and peaceful under the evening sky. I was shaking, shocked. My left hand had bits of greenish skin caught in the nails, with flecks of blood. I shoved my bare feet into my boots, picked up my clothes and ran back to the tent,

Two cups of hot sweet tea did wonders. Then my much-anticipated camping meal, but there was no way I could relax now. What on earth was living in that loch? 'Water-horses' were supposed to inhabit just about every loch in Scotland but that was sheer superstition. There was definitely nothing evil about the glen, or about the loch, the whole place had a very peaceful, natural feel to it. Whatever the creature was, it belonged there. Perhaps a super-giant trout??

Needless to say I didn't sleep well. A nearby stag was roaring but that didn't bother me, instead I had the distinct impression that little things were slithering past, round the tent, and when I did drop off I soon woke up again after a nightmare about dinosaurs. The wind had risen and sudden gusts shaking the tent did little for my peace of mind. Before first light I'd already breakfasted and as dawn rose, I began packing up ready to head back down the glen. So much for a relaxing night in the hills.

The sky was red, streaked with high cloud heralding approaching rain from the next Atlantic front. The air was full of the sound of the roaring of the rutting stags. The river level had fallen overnight, revealing a small beach of coarse sand just below the tent; when I went down to wash the breakfast pan I noticed that the sand had been churned up, it looked as if hundreds of eels had wriggled their way across it. Young eels, heading up into the hills to grow big in tributaries and lochs before the few survivors made their way back down to the sea. That must have been what I'd heard in the night. Then I noticed a couple of little creatures squirming down a peaty bank towards the beach. They were no eels.

The animals looked very strange indeed. Four flippers, like little legs, and a distinct triangular head joined to the main body by a long narrow neck. Strange, yet familiar. The stream by which I was camped was a tributary of a river which ran straight into Loch Ness...

Two days before I'd passed through Drumnadrochit with its model of the Loch Ness Monster peering out of the pond by one of the two rival exhibition centres. That model had been drawn from life. The secret glen was Nessie's spawning ground and nursery.

Connections

Someone has just won the lottery jackpot two weeks running! It's a chance of one in 40 trillion!'

'Wouldn't happen to me,' I replied, 'I've always found that the laws of probability work pretty well; if the chance is less one in a few hundred it never happens!'

I was down at the community office, catching up on some book-keeping and accounts. Great innovation, these places – takes the slog out of running a one-man (or in my case one-woman) business and gets you to meet others with the same problems. Sometimes I'd just go in for coffee, to have a natter and catch up with the local goings-on.

'In fact I think it sounds pretty suspicious.'

'That's what everybody's saying. But Grabbelot insists nobody can know the draw in advance and that it's just a fluke.'

'Who's the winner then?'

'They're trying to keep it secret, but the press are bound to find out soon!'

Sure enough, by evening the identity of the mysterious double-jackpot winner was on everyone's television screen; a crofter in the far north of Scotland. He wasn't giving away how he'd picked his winning numbers but reckoned he might now buy a new tractor.

The phone call came a few weeks later. Work had been very slack, and I'd been hoping for an enquiry or I'd normally have turned down this particular request straight away. Grabbelot would like me to come and talk to them. Not at their main headquarters – could be embarrassing if the press found out – they'd arrange a meeting room in some neutral offices just off Regent Street in London. No problem with paying my expenses and normal hourly rate. I'm always suspicious of organisations that don't like to be openly seen dealing with me – as if I'm into black magic – besides, the National Lottery wasn't my favourite organisation. I couldn't however really turn down work when it was in short supply. So armed with laptop computer I hopped onto the early morning train from Oxenholme to London and a few hours later walked into the offices in Charles II Street where we'd agreed to meet.

I was a little early and a receptionist took me up to the meeting room to wait. London offices can be surprisingly un-plush, and this one on the top floor had seen better days. The windows weren't even double glazed and had a view out over the roof-tops, washing was hanging outside a top-floor flat a few blocks away.

I had a surprise when the main Grabbelot delegation arrived. The Chief Executive himself was there with several technical people as well as a secretary or two; clearly this was something very important. I took my mind off the roof-top view and the washing and geared up for concentration.

We shook hands.

'Jack Baxter, Grabbelot. Pleased to meet you Miss Thomas.'

'Call me Lynne,' I replied. We sat down.

'Coffee?'

'Please. White with sugar.'

We exchanged the usual pleasantries about the weather, my journey, how I liked to live in the Cumbrian countryside and how it wasn't as remote as people thought. Then to business.

'As you probably realise,' began Jack, 'we have a problem – or we think we may have. We've been advised that you may be able to help us.'

I always like to make sure people understand what I do before we start. Some strange stories get around.

'You know my line of work?'

Jack hesitated, 'I have some idea, yes.'

'Specialist computer investigator. I sort out the really serious computer and network problems, when systems have been taken over by some hostile agent.'

Jack looked puzzled.

'Only computers? I was led to believe you had a, well, wider remit.'

Here we go again, I thought. Trust Grabbelot to think I'm some kind of witch doctor.

'Computer problems, that's my field. If your problems are more general than that I'm probably not your woman for the job. But let me know what the trouble is, and I'll soon tell you if I can be of any help.'

'This is all in strictest confidence, of course...'

I smiled to myself. People can get so embarrassed about religion, spirits, good and evil forces and such like. In this materialistic age, perhaps these things are the last taboo, so many folk cling desperately to the view that there is nothing other than the obvious physical world, in spite of all the evidence to the contrary. It's hard, as was said 2000 years ago, for a rich man to enter the kingdom of God, and most rich men prefer not to think too much about it.

Jack Baxter continued.

'You probably heard about the man who won the jackpot two weeks running. A staggeringly improbable occurrence. We're totally confident of our security over the lottery draw, but we investigated a bit further just to make quite sure there wasn't anything peculiar going on. We soon found out that there was. Peter, over to you.'

A middle-aged man with short beard stood up and switched on the computer projector.

'This map of the UK shows where the lottery winners have come from since the draws began. All wins over £10,000 are shown, I've used different colours to show the different sizes of win. As you might expect, wins are clustered around large centres of population.'

Indeed, at a first glance, the clusters of dots mirrored very well the locations and sizes of large cities. I noticed a few sparse dots across mid-Wales, Cumbria, the borders and the Scottish Highlands with a little cluster right on the far north coast near John O' Groats.

Peter put the next slide up.

'This map,' he went on, 'shows the location of lottery winners over the past year. As you can see, the distribution is still centred on large centres of population. See however this little cluster on the north coast of Scotland, it's comparable to these clusters over Manchester and Birmingham yet the population is tiny by comparison. OK, random distributions always give rise to clusters, we can do the statistics and it comes out fairly improbable, but not impossible, that the cluster is just chance. Now let me show you the wins over the last three months.'

The new map showed a sparse but fairly even distribution of dots except for the cluster in the far north of Scotland which dominated everything. I could count at least five red dots representing wins of over a million pounds, as well a dozen or so 'blue' wins of over a hundred thousand and maybe 20 or 30 black dots representing smaller prizes.

'We didn't believe this data when we first produced it. But it's right. There is no way that cluster could be chance. The probability comes out as about one in a googol – that's a "one" with a hundred zeros behind it. Something funny is going on.'

'Surely the local people in the area must have realised?'

'All winners refused publicity. It's only when that man won the jackpot two weeks on the trot that the locals have begun to cotton on that something's happening. Needless to say we've had people on the ground up there for the last few weeks investigating.'

'And?'

'We've found nothing illegal or suspicious. There are however some connections between the winners, and there you might be able to help. But we'll come onto that later. So – we have a cluster of lottery winners. Somehow we have to explain it and determine how people are beating the system. And soon, before the news gets more widely known. We'll then change our procedures in whatever way necessary to ensure fairness. We've eliminated chance. That's just too unlikely. Something else is at work here. Over to you again Peter.'

'We put a multi-disciplinary team together and brainstormed the problem. We collected the suggestions under the following headings. You'll understand of course that this must NOT get out to the press!'

As Peter was speaking I noticed, out of the window, that a lady was just hanging out more washing on top of the neighbouring building.

The projector slide listed a number of possibilities:

1. Corrupt selection of lottery balls, conjuring, trickery, etc.
2. Forgery of tickets after the draw.
3. Supercomputer prediction.
4. Time-travel.
5. Prophetic – dreams, visions, foretelling, etc.
6. Telekinetic influence on selection.
7. Parallel universes.
8. Other supernatural influence, devilry, black magic, etc.

'You might think that the first couple of options are the most likely, that someone is either somehow influencing the draw or forging winning tickets after the event. We can however guarantee our security procedures. It wouldn't help to go into details and for security reasons we'd rather not, but we know that nobody could interfere with the draw or fake a jackpot-winning ticket. We asked the Cambridge physicists and mathematicians for their opinions on 3,4 and 7. We didn't come away much the wiser but gathered that most scientists would rule out these options. Perhaps you'd care to investigate the possibilities yourself when you visit...'

'I've not yet said I'm willing to take on the job,' I retorted.

'We're sure you will. We can offer very attractive rates.'

I was sure they could. Immoral earnings, if you ask me, but then work was short.

'Then there is telekinesis – remote manipulation of objects. We approached the Edinburgh department of parapsychology and they basically laughed, they've some evidence of small effects but nothing that could influence a lottery draw. We've ruled out option 5 also; the jackpot would always be shared among hundreds if this was possible. So, we're left with magic and witchcraft which is where we reckon you may be able to help us...'

'I am NOT a witch or a magician, whatever tales you may have heard!'

'But you do know about such things. All the lottery winners have connections with the telecottage at a small north coast village called Strathy, and with the Dounreay nuclear power plant. So we do have reason to believe that computers are involved. We're willing to pay the going rate for your knowledge and skills. Just go up to Caithness for three weeks, see what you can find and we'll meet all your expenses.'

It was too tempting. Besides, I liked the Far North and it was about time I had another visit.

I booked a holiday cottage for three weeks, reckoning that I'd thereby preserve anonymity and be able to come and go as I pleased without attracting attention. It was late November, there were no tourists about and no difficulty in getting a three-star place. 'Puffin cottage' sounded good. Wintry weather had not yet set in; I'd have a leisurely drive up north, stopping over on the way for a bit of hill-walking.

It was turning towards dusk on a late Sunday afternoon as I drove my red Porsche through Helmsdale and began the climb over the twisty hills of the Ord of Caithness. Typical Caithness weather, a gale from the east, grey skies, rain spotting in the wind, the air misty with salt spray from the sea. After the final hairpin the road climbs up the hillside and rounds a bend to cross the summit of the Ord. Here on clear days are views to the Cairngorms nearly 100 miles away, with the sparkling sea far below. Here too, since before the days of planning regulations, has always been a huge signboard:

'Caithness Glass welcomes you to our county and factory at Wick'.

I glanced to the left, to see if the sign was still there – and very nearly put the car of the road. The sign had been changed.

'Caithness welcomes Lynne Thomas. Happy Birthday Lynne, 40 today!'

How on earth? I didn't notice much of the road for the next few miles. It couldn't be a coincidence. It WAS my birthday and I WAS 40, but nobody knew I was coming, or who I was or even worse, how old I was, indeed I'd thought that one of my better kept secrets. As dark fell I continued over the CausewayMire road towards Thurso in a bit of a daze. It must have been the owner of the cottage I'd booked or perhaps that Regent Street office had been bugged, maybe that woman hanging out the washing had something to do with it. So much for anonymity.

The holiday cottage was just a few miles out of Thurso and owned by a Mrs Sinclair, a nice lady in her mid-forties, who let me in and showed me round. It was all clean and well-equipped, very warm in spite of the easterly gale and I was assured that the view would be magnificent in daylight and clear weather. I explained that I was up on business for three weeks but hoped to take a few days off exploring the area, perhaps even do a bit of cycling if the weather wasn't too bad. Yes, I could borrow a bike if I wanted, her husband was a keen cyclist and cycled the 15 miles to work every day.

'I've left a local paper out for you,' she said as she gave me the keys, 'people often like to know what's going on in the county.'

A teapot and a plate of shortbread had been thoughtfully provided, I made myself a cup, took a bite from a shortbread finger, picked up the paper, sat down, and nearly choked. My own face was staring at me from the front page of the *John O' Groat Journal*, next to the headline 'Famous witchdoctor visits Caithness.'

The article, when I'd steeled myself to read it, was actually remarkably accurate and unbiased but goodness knows where they had got the information from. I was attractive, blonde and 40, an expert in exorcism of computers (a recent and growing problem, I was told) and visiting Caithness to investigate the recent cluster of lottery wins. I was expected to visit Dounreay and the telecottage at Strathy among other venues (that was the first I knew about it). There followed what could have been a shortened transcript of the London meeting, explaining that Grabbelot had decided on magic and witchcraft as the most likely explanation and had called me in. There was even a leader article to the effect that I was very welcome to the Far North but would uncover nothing sinister. The locals were fully entitled to benefit from their enterprise in devising winning lottery strategies and I should take this message back to Grabbelot.

Somehow that secret London meeting had been leaked. I plugged my laptop into the phone socket and sent an urgent fax down to Grabbelot. An hour or two later the reply came back: 'Carry on with your investigations.'

My cover was well and truly blown, I'd just have to make the best of it.

Everyone would be expecting me to start work the next day. I'd surprise them. A day off wouldn't be a bad idea after the long journey. I'd have a bike ride out into the flow country then come down into Strathy from the moors, take a look round as an inconspicuous and anonymous cyclist and pedal back in the dark. That way I'd get a feel for the place without being recognised. The forecast was good, I went round to Mrs Sinclair and borrowed her husband's mountain bike for the following day.

To make sure nobody saw me I decided to catch the early morning train which left the local station of Georgemas Junction at around seven; I'd alight 30 minutes later in Forsinard. So very early on Monday morning saw me pedalling down the hill in the dark; it was four miles to the station and I was leaving plenty of time. Shortly after I'd turned onto the main road I noticed a light coming up behind me, another cyclist had caught me up. A man slowed up and cycled alongside. 'Grand morning for a ride!'

I agreed.

'I'm Alex Sinclair – you'll have met my wife Anne – we own Puffin Cottage.'

'That's right,' I replied, 'I'm Lynne. I believe this is your mountain bike?'

'Yes, it's actually not bad,' he replied, 'a bit slow on roads though. Going far?'

I mentioned that I was getting the train out to Forsinard then heading across the moors to Strathy.

'Good for you! We don't get many in the cottage who are so adventurous! Mind you look in at the bothy if you're going that way, I'm one of those who looks after it! Anyway I've got to leave you now, I turn right here towards Halkirk. I'll be thinking of you out enjoying the fresh air and sunshine when I'm stuck in my Dounreay office. See you!'

And with that he headed off towards the orange lights of Halkirk village, a mile or two away.

'I wonder,' thought Alex as he approached the level crossing where the Halkirk road crossed the railway, 'not strictly legal but then it's Donny on the train this morning...'

I had a few minutes to wait at the station before the little two-coach sprinter came rattling in out of the dark. The guard got down to help me with the bike and before I could say a word began,

'Morning Lynne – Forsinard is it?'

At least the train was almost empty and nobody else seemed to recognise me. At Forsinard it was still only just getting light, the sky was clear and there was a slight frost. It looked a good day for an adventurous route; I'd take the track to Greamachary then wheel the bike for some seven or eight miles across the lochan-strewn flow country of Sutherland to the remote Loch Strathy bothy. A long track would then take me down to Strathy followed by a 25 mile ride back to Puffin Cottage on roads.

The train gave a 'toot-toot' as it rattled out of the station towards Kinbrace and silence descended. I mounted the bike and pedalled off southwards, soon warming up and enjoying the ride, over a low pass towards the dawn sky. There was complete silence, the growing light reflecting from the flow-country pools below the road. No-one was about as I turned down the two-mile track to the isolated fishing bothy at Greamachary, the bike crunching through thin ice on the track and splashing through deeper puddles as a herd of deer scattered in the early morning half-light below a sky streaked with red streamers of high cloud.

There was a light on at the cottage; I groaned inwardly, it was still the hind-stalking season and I might be rudely turned back. Perhaps I could sneak past – but no, a man was coming down to meet me.

I slowed and stopped. 'Lovely morning,' I said in as friendly a voice as possible.

'Grand,' the man replied. 'Pleased to meet you, Lynne. Fancy a cup of tea before you carry on?'

This was going to take some getting used to.

Hours later, after a wetter, rougher crossing than I'd expected I wheeled the bike across the last knoll beyond Loch an Saobhaidhe and down through the heather towards the forest fence and the bothy. I was by now not over-surprised to see smoke coming from the bothy chimney, even though it was one of the remotest in Scotland.

Sure enough when I opened the door of the empty house the fire was lit, a kettle on it was boiling, tea and sugar were laid out but nobody was there. A little note simply read: 'Welcome, Lynne, to the Croft House, make yourself at home.'

So the day went on. A banner was stretched across the track, six miles down towards Strathy by an isolated log-cabin: 'Happy Birthday, Lynne'.

After some 11 or 12 miles of churned up, bumpy track the tarmac started, just south of Strathy village and here was another banner:

'Strathy welcomes Lynne Thomas'. So much for entering the

village by the back route. I didn't bother cycling around, anonymously and inconspicuously, I might as well drive there in my bright red Porsche the next morning.

I hadn't realised until then that a strong south-easterly wind had been picking up, and into this I had to push, mostly in the dark, for the long 25 miles back to the cottage. Almost every car that passed toot-tooted me. It was starting to rain on the long grind up the hills from Thurso into what was now a near gale – then I saw that light on the road again from another cyclist. It was Alex Sinclair, on his way home from work. 'Fine night!' he called out as he overtook at speed, his red rear light rapidly disappearing ahead. Oh well. At least I was being well paid.

The following morning I donned my neatest suit, got into my plush car and drove out to Strathy. There didn't seem to be much point in making an appointment to visit the telecottage as everyone in the north of Scotland knew I'd be coming. The weather had turned colder, a front had come through overnight and there were a couple of nasty squalls of hail on the drive across.

As I walked in the door of the building a young man got up from a computer screen.

'Pleased to meet you again, Lynne. Actually I was expecting you, my brother's secretary said you'd be coming!'

'Your brother's secretary?'

'Her sister's partner works in London, he was taking the tea and biscuits into a meeting in Regent Street, overheard them talking about Caithness and couldn't resist listening a bit longer. Do you remember me?'

So that was how the grapevine had worked. Oh well. The man looked familiar – it's always so difficult to recognise somebody you've met in totally different circumstances – then I realised with delight who it was.

'Norman! We met at Gorm Choire bothy a few years ago! I'd always hoped to meet you again!'

'Same here! I always wondered how you managed to get back

in that weather. I must say at the time I thought you were off your rocker, it's only since then that I realised that your line of business really is genuine!'

I'd met Norman by chance at a remote bothy in wild weather a few years before, and had rather surprised him by performing a bit of unexpected exorcism. The return trip from the bothy had indeed been a bit of a struggle with a bike across hills deep in slushy snow amid gales of rain. We chatted about hills and bothies for a few minutes before I managed to turn the conversation to my reason for calling in.

'You'll know why I'm here?'

'Like everyone else in the area, yes. You're suspicious of our lottery system'

'You do have a system?'

'There is one, yes. You'll have to talk to somebody else about that but I'll be surprised if they let you know how it works. I can assure you though that everything's above board, no supernatural influences here. This is, after all, the heart of Free Presbyterian country!'

'Well, I can quickly check that for myself if you let me onto your computers.'

'The floor's yours but mind, these aren't just ordinary PCs!'

'It's OK,' I said, 'I'm qualified to deal with any system and have run checks on the largest and most prestigious of companies...'

'Well, we have the most powerful computer in Scotland. We took it over when Dounreay scrapped it.'

'Scrapped it?'

'Typical Dounreay. Ditched a top-notch CFD research program, sacked the staff and we got the computers as scrap, all because Harwell in the south of England was jealous. That's when I gave up and went part-time...'

It didn't take long to carry out the checks. I plugged in my laptop and ran the usual battery of tests on the network. The system was totally clean.

'Is the lottery software mounted?' I asked.

'Couldn't say,' replied Norman. 'Perhaps you should talk to Davie Mackay about that. Take the road out to Strathy East, just past where they're building the new old folks' home and it's the last house on the left.'

'Davie's not the one who won the jackpot twice running, is he?'

'The very same! But you'll find him very nice. Doing a lot for the area, our Davie!'

It was only half a mile to Davie's house at the end of the road, a very ordinary croft house, usual rusting van, pile of creels and peat-stack, just a shiny new tractor looking a bit out of place.

I knocked. 'Come in, Lynne,' came a friendly voice from inside. 'Door's open.' By now I was used to being recognised by everybody I'd never met before.

The house was nicely modernised but the main room still had a big old fireplace with a fire of glowing peat and a kettle hanging over it.

'You'll have a cup of tea? Sorry I can't offer you anything stronger on a cold morning like this but I've been teetotal all my 71 years.' Seventy-one? He looked about 50.

'That'll suit me fine,' I replied, 'I don't imbibe either and besides I'm driving. You'll know why I'm here?'

Davie didn't seem to hear the question and carried on talking as he removed the kettle from the fire and poured the boiling water into an old china teapot.

'Would it have been you I saw coming past yesterday on a bicycle? It can't have been a very good day for a bicycle! Used to cycle in to Dounreay myself till I retired.'

'You worked at Dounreay then? What was your line?'

Davie threw a couple more peats on the fire.

'Reactor shift manager, that's until they shut the reactor down! Nuclear energy runs in the family. My young son's in charge of Metropolitan Edison Inc. in the States while my eldest daughter's the station manager of Wylfa on Anglesey.'

A bright lot, these north coast folk. I decided not to ask what the other members of Davie's family were doing.

'So,' I said, 'now about the lottery...'

'You'll have seen the new old folks' home? Due to open in the middle of next year.'

I mentioned that I'd noticed the construction site.

'We'd been trying to get the Highland Council to build one for years but they're just not interested in anything outside Inverness or the Western Isles, so we in the local community decided to pay for it ourselves. We've also set up a trust fund to run it. Lottery money you see.'

'You mean from the Charities Fund?'

'No, they turned the proposal down. You know, farming's in a very bad way up here just now.'

'Farming?'

Davie continued

'Farmers and crofters are getting nothing for their lambs, beef prices are rock bottom and after the dreadful summer there's little or no winter feed. They need a boost. Milk and sugar?'

I took the offered mug and sipped the hot, slightly peat-smoke flavoured brew. A sudden squall had risen, the wind was roaring around the house, hail hammered on the window while occasional pellets came down the chimney, melting on the hearth to leave little black circles of soot.

'So I decided to do something about it. Every farmer and crofter in the Far North is getting a Christmas present of a cheque for £2000. Had to get a special delivery of cheque-books from the bank.'

I tried to bring the subject back to the lottery system but every time Davie had a way of diverting attention. I gathered that apart from his new tractor, all his winnings were going on worthy causes in the Far North. I heard story after story about local village life, about the Bettyhill postie, about the problems in the church. Finally, after about two hours, he suddenly came to the point.

'Must go out now and check that the tups are doing their job – if you want to find out more about the lottery system you could do worse than try Mrs Sinclair who runs the guest house just along the road. Ever tried the lottery yourself?'

I confessed that I didn't approve of it.

'You're being paid by Grabbelot now, and that's much the same thing! All our winnings go to charity. Birthdays, now. They always reckon that birthdays are good ways of picking winning numbers. I'd try birthdays if I were you!'

To cut a long story short, I spent the rest of the day talking to extremely nice, friendly people who all had at least one substantial lottery win to their credit but were giving no secrets away. Always I was passed onto somebody else who might be able to help. I finally gave up when it was suggested that I go and see Davie Mackay. What seemed clear was that there was a system, that somebody (probably Norman, I reckoned) ran some software which predicted the numbers, and that the winnings were all spent on local charitable causes.

Most local people were not well off and even Dounreay wages were nothing special. I was beginning to feel a little guilty at being paid top consultant daily rates which were more than many locals would earn in a month.

During the rest of the week I got nowhere. Several times I dropped in at Strathy unannounced, only to discover that the local grapevine already knew I was on my way. Once I walked along the clifftops from Melvich, only to meet a shepherd at Baligill who greeted me: 'Good morning, Miss Thomas.' Never did my checks of the telecottage computers uncover anything suspicious or supernatural.

Saturday, I decided, would be a day off; I drove west and climbed Ben Hope, the summit was wild with a gale of sleet and for once I met nobody. I was back early, a good thing as the rain was turning to wet sleet even at low levels. That evening, back at the cottage, I watched the televised lottery draw, not a thing I'd normally do but then I did have a professional interest...

The numbers came out, one by one. 29, 11, 19, 5, 9, 40.

There was something familiar about those numbers. 29/11 – that was my birthday. A coincidence in view of what the man at Strathy had said – wait a minute, 1959 – that was the year of my birth! and I was 40!

I am, perhaps, more used to dealing with strange and inexplicable occurrences than most people. But this was a bit much. How on earth?

At that moment, all the lights went out.

I had, vaguely, noticed that the gale-driven wet sleet was starting to build up on the windows. Somewhere in a cupboard were candles and matches. First to grope my way in the dark through the kitchen. There was a knock at the door, and a light. I made my way into the porch and after fumbling with the key managed to undo the lock; there was Alex Sinclair, plastered in wet snow after just the 50 yard walk from his own front door.

'I'm afraid the power's off, as you probably noticed! In this sort of weather the wet snow freezes on the lines and brings them down, it could be a few days before it comes back on, I'm afraid. You'd better be coming round and staying with us; we've got solid fuel heating but it will get very cold in this cottage!'

I thanked him for the offer and agreed that, if the power was still off the next day, I might take him up on it. Meanwhile he lent me a Tilley lamp and some extra candles.

By morning the house was cold and dismal and the hot water had run out. It was blowing a blizzard of fine snow, visibility out of the windows was a few yards and deep drifts would be blocking the road. Alex called again to see if I was OK and this time I agreed it would be better to stay with them until things improved. Outside it was really wild, the sort of weather I'd only met before on mountain-tops, and I was glad to enter the warmth of the Sinclair's house with a roaring coal fire.

'Sorry about this,' said Anne Sinclair, 'it happens almost every year. No good relying on electricity here in the winter! You'll have lunch with us?'

I thanked her for her offer. 'We've baked potatoes doing in the ash-pan, a gammon joint cooking on the fire, sprouts from the garden.'

'Picked at great personal risk in the storm,' interjected Alex.

Over dinner, as the spindrift whirled outside the double-glazing, the conversation turned to my lottery investigations. Alex burst out laughing at my description of the evasive Strathy folk. 'They'd never tell you! I know Davie well, used to work for me before he retired. Anyway I know how they do it...'

'Alex!' scolded Anne.

'It's nothing illegal or supernatural, just a way of bringing some much needed funding to our scattered communities. There's no way though you'll ever find the secret while you're in the pay of Grabbelot!'

'So you do know how the system works?'

'Yes, actually. Not that I'd tell anyone, or use it myself – a touch immoral in my view.'

'Last night the winning numbers were my birthday!'

'Oh no!' laughed Anne, 'typical Norman trick!'

'Anne!' scolded Alex.

'So it's Norman! And he must be influencing the draw! How on earth does he do that? Are you sure there's no witchcraft involved?'

'No witchcraft,' said Alex, 'just the laws of physics. And mathematics. But I'm afraid it's only going to work for another three weeks before the Millennium puts paid to it.'

'Come on! You just said it was the laws of physics. How can a purely artificial date be built into natural laws?'

'Now, that would be telling...'

We were just finishing our tea when there was a hammering on the front door.

'Not expecting visitors in this weather!' said Alex, getting up to see. We both went with him. Drifts had already piled up against the outer door and snow fell inwards as a completely snow-plastered and encrusted figure stepped into the porch, he stamped hard to shake off the worst of the snow then came into the kitchen. It was Norman from Strathy!

'Hi Alex,' he began, 'phones are off so I had to get to Thurso and thought I'd come round while I was there. No good in the car with all the roads blocked so came on the bike, but it took me five hours, the drifts must be eight feet deep just along the road and I had to wheel it most of the way – why, hello Lynne, nice to see you!'

Fifteen minutes later, Norman had changed into dry clothes and we were all sitting round the blazing fire.

'Remember that this woman,' said Anne, 'is in the pay of Grabbelot'

'WAS in the pay of Grabbelot.' I interjected. 'I've decided. All you lot up here are far more deserving of Lottery money than those on the Grabbelot board who only want to buy themselves another yacht. As soon as the phones are back I'll call them up and tell them to forget their job and their money. I'll stay up here and go skiing and see in the Millennium. And you can keep your secrets. I've had enough of prying and questioning everyone, I'd much rather just be friends!'

'Wait a minute,' said Norman, 'could we not come to some arrangement? How much were Grabbelot paying you?'

'£25,000,' I admitted, shamefaced.

'You don't want to turn down that sort of money. Our winnings are going to stop in three weeks time anyway. Tell you what. If you put half your earnings into the new hospice at Wick and keep our secret for another three weeks, we'll tell you how we do it. You just tell them that you've found out how its done, that it's a professional secret but that the abnormal winnings will cease with the Millennium!'

'Done!' I said. 'But I'll put all the money into the local charities. You never know, I might decide to move up here myself!'

'That would be nice,' said Norman. 'What I was really coming here to say,' he continued, 'was that I managed to get the winning numbers confirmed from Thurso. We don't yet know if anybody else has shared the jackpot but we should have enough now to pay for a new breakwater at Wick.'

'Didn't Stevenson try to build one in the nineteenth century and fail?'

'That's true, but with modern technology it's perfectly possible if you've got enough money!'

'SO,' I said, 'how *does* your system work?'

'Have you got your laptop computer with you?'

I reckoned that the batteries would last a couple of hours.

'Right,' said Alex, 'I'll get the floppy.'

'You know about quantum mechanics?' asked Norman.

'A bit, yes.'

'Well you probably know of the weird effect where two or more particles can become 'entangled' when close together; this entanglement then remains even if the particles are separated by the entire universe, provided that nothing interferes with either of them.'

'A bit like love which remains even when a couple is apart?'

'Quite a bit like that, yes,' said Norman, smiling and looking straight at me. He continued.

'Looking at one of the particles is a bit liking asking the woman if she wants to marry, she's forced to make her mind up and this immediately affects the man. So it is with these entangled particles, even if they are light-years apart. By looking at one particle I can force the other particle to adopt a particular position. I discovered that something like this can be used to influence the lottery draw.'

'How on earth do you manage that?'

'The draw's completely random, Grabbelot make sure of that, so the principles of quantum mechanics apply. Let me demonstrate. I'll load this floppy into your laptop – a neat little machine indeed – then run the programme.'

The disc drive whirred briefly and a familiar picture of black circles and wavy coloured patterns appeared on the screen.

' Oh no!' I exclaimed, 'Not a Mandelbrot! Don't tell me you're going anywhere near 666!'

'Don't worry, I know about that! Now what year is it?'

'1999, of course.'

'You realise that 1999 is a prime number. 2000 isn't. So we have 1999 subsidiary buds of period 1999 on the main Mandelbrot bud which we can visit in turn...'

'You what???'

'Don't worry about the details. Just remember that what I'm doing didn't work in 1998 and won't work in 2000 simply because 1999 is a different sort of number – I'm afraid this particular Millennium bug can't be avoided. Now watch as I get one of the "period 1999" buds on the screen.'

Norman clicked the mouse and, very slowly, another Mandelbrot pattern with a central black circle ringed by smaller circles, wavy lines and spirals started to appear.

'Not quite got the power of our Strathy set-up, this machine – anyway I now follow the wiggly main branch up from the end of the new "period 1999" bud and home in on the largest of the little Mandelbrot shapes that follow, one after another. You get the idea. The Mandelbrot set is so vast that you can almost guarantee that nobody in the world has looked at this part of it before, that's crucial. I can choose to look at whichever buds I like, and I've a wee program which tells me what the periods will be before I look at them. Purely by chance I discovered that when I'd looked at six buds, these came up as the following week's winning lottery numbers! So I could influence the draw at will. Last week I chose to look at the side buds off the "period 1999" buds which corresponded to your birthday and age – sorry about that, you really don't look 40 – and printed them out. For some reason there is a quantum entanglement with the lottery balls. It doesn't always work perfectly, probably because someone in the past, somewhere in the universe has already looked at one of the little buds. On those weeks we only get four or five numbers right.'

'But what other entanglements are hidden in the Mandelbrot set, what else is altered when you look at it?'

'Who knows? Maybe the whole of world history is there, maybe it's the 21st Century crystal ball if we can but decode it. But I think there's a more important entanglement we should sort out. Fancy coming to the Millennium Ceilidh in the Strathy Hall?'

The beast of 4.669

A perfectly ordinary business park in industrial north-west England, a perfectly ordinary company headquarters, a perfectly extra-ordinary murder – or was it suicide – or what?

The gory death had occurred at the UK headquarters of PC Solutions, a world-wide specialist software and computer solutions company. The seven-storey Y-shaped building overlooked a carpark in a wall of glass-fronted offices and housed some 1500 staff. 'You've got a computer problem, we can solve it for you,' was their motto – and they did, very successfully.

The meeting had been turning into an all-night sitting. The Chairman of the Board, Jim Watson, had failed to return after a 10pm coffee break. Somebody noticed blood trickling from a locked cubical in the men's toilets. The door was broken open and Jim was found dead, sitting on the toilet, his shirt and jacket soaked in blood. There was no sign of a struggle. There was no weapon. Nobody had heard or seen anything unusual. Forensics confirmed that he'd been killed while sitting on the toilet, that he'd died as a result of a single, huge, stab-wound through the heart. Why had he not moved, or struggled? How had an assailant killed him through the locked door and escaped without leaving any traces of blood? The wound indicated a most unusual weapon, a very pointed knife with vicious barbs and spikes mounted on the blade.

It was 11 April, 2001.

The lack of a struggle made the police think that Jim Watson might have known his assailant who had, perhaps, been invited into the cubicle for 'a bit on the side'. OK – a strange thing for a top man to do in the middle of a meeting – but there have been weirder perversions among senior people. It didn't however fit his character; he'd been married for 25 years, happily as far as everyone knew, with two grown-up children and a teenage daughter – but then men have their secrets.

So police suspicions initially centred on those at the meeting who'd taken a natural break at the same time as him.

Jim had been seen to go into a cubicle and close the door. Others had been talking and had left the toilets together. Perhaps somebody had used a pre-arranged signal to join Jim. There were, however, no indications of any anyone else being there and nobody could have committed such a violent crime without being spattered in blood.

The cubicle shared a common wall with a secretarial office which had been locked and in darkness. There was no hidden entry to the cubicle from there or from any other side, above or below. The assailant must have entered through the door, left the same way – *and locked the door behind him* (or her). There was a small gap under and above the door but not nearly enough for anyone to squeeze through. The toilets were on the top floor and while a determined cat burglar might have managed to climb up from the outside there were no signs of forced entry.

It turned out that the door couldn't easily be locked from the outside. It was quite easy to unlock using bit of plastic, but a specially constructed tool was needed to lock it again. Why should the assailant have bothered?

Needless to say the security staff had seen or heard nothing suspicious, nor had any other staff who had been working late. So there it was. Jim Watson leaves the late-evening meeting with a group of others to visit the toilet. He goes into a cubicle. At some point somebody else joins him, presumably invited as there was no struggle, and suddenly stabs him with a particularly nasty barbed knife. The assailant leaves quietly, somehow locking the door behind him, and either calmly rejoins the meeting (without any sign of bloodstains and having hidden his weapon) or else slips out of the building unseen.

The police searched the building and grounds, for days. They didn't find the weapon. All the video camera recordings were checked. Nothing. Everyone who'd been in the building was interviewed; there was absolutely nothing suspicious.

A few months later the mysterious attacker struck again.

20 July, 2001. People arriving for work discovered a pool of partly congealed blood spreading from under the door of a locked toilet cubicle on the second floor. Inside was the body of Ben Stephens, a young systems programmer. The circumstances were very similar to those of Jim Watson's death. Same, unusual, vicious weapon. Locked door. No sign of a struggle. Stabbed through the heart. Time of death around 10pm the night before. He'd been working late on a project to meet a tight deadline. He was heterosexual with a steady partner with whom he lived, and had no known deviant behaviour.

Indeed it was exactly 100 days since the previous murder. That it had taken place at the same time of day, with few people in the building, perhaps had some significance. But the police were baffled. Once again they had forensics crawling over every inch of the place. Everybody was interviewed. There were no leads, no clues, nothing. Several dozen people had been in the building on both occasions but there were no grounds for suspecting any individual. Reluctantly, the management and unions agreed to video cameras being installed in all the toilets. Security was tightened. A 'buddy' system was brought in for people working outside normal hours. There was little else the police could do but keep the files open and hope for more information. Everybody working in the building was jittery, not without good reason...

11 August 2001. 8am. The company worked flexitime and a growing trickle of people had been arriving for work since before seven. Two male employees were walking down the corridor towards their office on the third floor, in graphics, when they

heard an agonised female scream, cut terribly short, from the office they were just passing. They burst in the door to discover a young lady – one of the designers – lying on the floor next to an overturned office chair, blood spurting from her chest. One of the young men, trained in first aid, grabbed a cushion and tried to stifle the flow of blood but it was obvious he could do little. She was still just conscious 'What happened – who did it...' ' Man...' she struggled to speak then, with a little groan, died.

Others were soon on the scene, having heard the scream and seen the two men burst into the office.

The office was small, with one door. The men would have seen anyone leaving. Other witnesses testified that they had heard the scream before the men burst into the office. The window was closed, and too small for anyone to gain entry. There was nowhere for anyone to hide, there was nowhere even to hide a weapon, especially one as terrible as that used for the murder.

It had to be a conspiracy. When you eliminate the impossible... Perhaps the girl screamed as a signal, the men burst in, murdered her, hid the weapon somehow – but why? There was no motive. Neither of the two men could be implicated in the previous killings.

Perhaps a secret group of people in the building had a strange suicide pact. Medical opinion considered that it would be difficult but not impossible to inflict such injuries upon oneself. But what had happened to the weapon? Detective stories invoke daggers made out of ice or solid carbon dioxide but in the latest death, such a device would not have had time to melt or evaporate before the two men appeared on the scene, unless of course they were involved in the murder. The last word of the girl, if you could believe the testimony of the two men (who were perfectly ordinary people of known good character) was 'man', but all the evidence was that the girl was on her own, nobody could have hidden or escaped without being seen.

It could only be a bizarre suicide pact using some unknown

weapon which evaporated in seconds. The evidence had to be stretched to the limit to fit the theory but there seemed little alternative. Forensic and other experts were extremely skeptical that the injuries could have been inflicted by anything other than a very specialist device, a dagger with a fine spike and numerous barbs, a carefully engineered and finely honed weapon, nothing that could be crudely fashioned out of ice, solid nitrogen or anything similar. But where was it?

The detective in charge of the case was stuck, baffled, and so was everybody else. The company was now suffering badly, most employees had walked out and refused to resume work until the killer was found. This, the third mysterious death in six months, made the national headlines.

PC Solutions Inc. suspected a vendetta and decided to move out before anything else happened. They announced the closure of their UK headquarters with the loss of 1500 jobs. Speculation was that the building would have to be demolished.

It was after the third death that I started wondering. That 100 day interval between the first and second murder stirred something in my subconscious. I had a crazy hunch and checked it out on the calculator and with that familiar sinking feeling realised that indeed it was my kind of problem, that another death was due soon, that like it or not I'd have to get involved...

I phoned Jack Taylor, the man in charge of the case, as soon as I could get him. He'd had a long, frustrating day, had never heard of me and reckoned I was a crank. When I suggested it could be some kind of computer bug problem he told me that computer bugs didn't murder people. I replied that they did, and had – but he said he couldn't afford the time for an interview.

I could only plead with him. 'I hope I'm wrong – but I think the next death is due to occur just after 10pm on 15 August. Please, please make sure the building's empty then...'

I hoped sincerely I was wrong but had a horrible feeling that I was right.

At 6am on 16 August I phoned Jack Taylor again. I knew that if I was right he'd already be up and working on the case.

'Has anything happened?' I asked.

'What kind of thing?' he replied, casually.

'Dammit – has someone else been killed – look you MUST let me help if there's been another murder – or someone else may die tonight!'

'Stay right there,' he replied, 'don't try anything. The police are on on their way to you now!'

At that, I'm afraid I burst out laughing..

'I'm not the murderer! You should have called me in ages ago. I'm the only person who might be able to clear this up for you. Just ask anyone about the KAA case or...'

'I think you'd better come and tell us what you know about this... I'll send a police car round to collect you.'

'That won't be much good – I live in the far north of Scotland! How about a fast jet to pick me up from Wick airport?'

'Wick? Where's that? Look I'll have to speak to my boss. I'll get back to you.'

Apparently when Jack contacted his boss at 6.30am he was told in no uncertain terms to get me there as fast as possible, my reputation was well known in the higher echelons.

At 8am I boarded a plush executive jet in Wick for the half-hour flight down to Manchester where a police car was waiting to whisk me at 100mph, siren wailing, down the motorway. Shortly after nine I was ushered into an urgently convened meeting on the Risley Business Park just outside Warrington.

Chief Inspector Tony Parker briefly outlined the history of the case, much of which I already knew from the newspaper and TV reports. Then he came to the latest 'development'.

'PC Solutions have been employing armed security guards to patrol at night. A particularly fit, tough young man failed to return from his patrol and could not be contacted on his radio or mobile phone. He was found, dead, in a corridor on the fourth floor. He'd been stabbed by the same weapon as had killed the other three. There was no sign of a struggle. He'd obviously made no effort to draw a gun or a knife. He died at around ten yesterday evening as you predicted. I'd appreciate it if you can explain how you came to know the time of the crime in advance.'

'Could you first confirm the precise dates and times when the murders took place?' I asked.

I quickly entered the times into my pocket calculator as he spoke and did a few divisions. It was as I'd suspected and feared.

'Does the number 4.669 mean anything to you?'

Both men shook their heads, puzzled.

'I won't explain the mathematical significance of that number now. But look at the times between the murders. The first one was 466.9 days after midnight on 31 December 1999. The second was exactly 100 days later. The third was 21.4 days (that's 100 divided by 4.669) after that. The last was another 4.58 days – (21.4 divided by 4.669) later – as I'd predicted if you remember. If the pattern continues we're due another in just 0.98 days (that's 4.58 divided by 4.669) or 23.5 hours after the last, in other words at around 9.42pm this evening.'

'You mean – you reckon somebody else is due to die tonight?'

'Yes. And then at 2.45am. And then at 3.53, at 4.07 at 4.10 and at increasingly frequent intervals after that. If there's nobody in the building I wouldn't care to speculate what might happen but we could see deaths spreading out into the area around – or across the computer network throughout the world – it could get very nasty or even apocalyptic at around four o' clock tomorrow morning!'

'Hang on – we're just looking for a murderer!' interjected Jack.

'It's a lot worse than that,' I replied. 'I've seen this sort of thing before. To be blunt I suspect an evil force in the computer system. My speciality is in dealing with such things.'

'But...' Jack began.

'Jack,' said Tony, 'Lynne knows what she's talking about. She's helped us before. Lynne – if you're right time is short. Do you want to visit the PC Solutions building immediately?'

'As soon as possible. But I'm only human. I could do with a coffee and a bite to eat first – and you must trust me Jack, I'm the only person equipped for this!'

I better had be. This one looked really nasty and there was no time to bring in anyone else to help.

We walked across the business park to the PC Solutions building. It had been the headquarters of some government establishment until the Thatcher era and looked just like it; seven storeys of paper-pushing offices overlooking a large and now empty car-park. We reported to a Portacabin, a security man came out and unlocked the main door of the eerily empty headquarters building for us.

I'd been expecting a horrible atmosphere and my expectations were fully realised; I could immediately feel that something very evil was lurking in that building. Most computers were switched off but the building held vital international network servers and these were still in use, albeit operated via remote terminals. I preferred not to think of the possible consequences if I didn't clear the problem by the late evening.

'Can't you just turn off the power?' asked Jack.

'Very dangerous,' I replied, 'that could simply force the evil out onto any of or all of the networked computers, giving us a still bigger problem to contend with. Besides, unless the computers and discs are completely destroyed, the evil will just come back in full strength when the power is turned on again. No, I'll have to deal with it here while the machines are running. If you don't mind – could we start in the graphics department where that poor girl was killed?'

The Paternoster lifts were switched off, so we walked up the echoing stairwell overlooking a courtyard at the back of the building, a courtyard already becoming overgrown with weed. At the third floor Jack slipped a security pass into the reader, typed in a number and opened the door leading to the offices. The evil was stronger here, I said a quick prayer, silently, and followed him down the corridor. The forces of good are always stronger but even I need to keep reminding myself of this.

The fatal office had been cleaned and tidied up and looked just like any other. Good, the computers were still there and plugged in. I sat down at a convenient PC and turned on the power.

I'd been hoping to feel an increased feeling of evil emanating from the machine as it came up but there wasn't anything. It booted up normally, with that dreadful Microsoft jingle most out-of-place in the circumstances. The machine was still networked to the servers. I plugged in my laptop and began to send agents round the system probing, checking...

The results were what I'd feared. There was no specific problem I could latch onto. There was definitely something, or some Thing, deep in the system but it was avoiding confrontation, hiding. Perhaps if I'd had Don to help I might have been able to pin it down – but whatever it was simply retreated before my exorcism codes, regrouping in another corner of the system.

We tried the main computer room. I had to force myself to go in the door, so strong was the feeling of evil emanating outwards. The two men I was with noticed nothing. But even when I had my laptop plugged into the main console machine, there was nothing I could do. This was going to be a slippery customer.

'I need a bit of time to think,' I said. 'I could also do with some fresh air!'

The feeling of relief, of release, on leaving the building was incredible. But I knew I'd have to go back, I'd feared this from the start but had hoped things might not be as bad.

The only way I could hope to overcome the problem would be to enter the building alone and to be sitting at that console at 9.30pm that evening when the next person was due to die. And to make sure that person wasn't me.

Needless to say it took some persuading before the police would let me even try. They finally agreed on condition that they did a thorough search of the building beforehand and posted armed guards at all possible entrances. I stressed that it was absolutely vital that I was the only person in the building; I could look after myself (I assured them) but anyone else could die. Fortunately Tony had worked with me before and knew about these things, Jack however wasn't at all happy.

'Look,' I told him, 'if I'm right about the timings of the deaths then it's my kind of problem and only I can deal with it. If I'm wrong and these actually are conventional murders then you'll have nothing to worry about if you know nobody else is in the building.' My logic was at last grudgingly accepted.

The last word of the third victim. The nature of the weapon. 4.669. I now knew the kind of Thing I was dealing with.

I'd dealt with many such problems before, I knew the powers of good to be stronger than those of evil. I'd many years of experience, but this didn't make me any more eager to re-enter that building in the late evening. I'm only human. I knew the good God. I knew that many of my ancestors in the same general line of business had faced worse, without the benefits of modern technology. When it comes to the crunch you just ignore your emotions and feelings. There was a job to do. I would do it. I'd survive, even if it killed me.

It was a windy, overcast night. The roads were quiet as we drove out to the Risley Business park. Tony accompanied me to the door. He shook my hand. 'Good luck. Lynne, you know best!'

It was nine o'clock.

I let the door close and lock behind me.

All the corridor lights had been left on, it could almost have been a late winter afternoon but for the empty passageways and offices. The main computer room was on the ground floor, I just had to pass through a couple of key-card operated security doors to reach it. The feeling of evil was strong, but no stronger than before.

I said a prayer before I sat down at the console computer and plugged in my laptop. Yes, the powers of good would win. But it could be a hard fight and there was a danger, even for me – when the battle gets tough one can be accidentally trampled underfoot.

This time my software agents were meeting some resistance. Something was developing, as I'd thought it would; there were just 15 minutes to go. Little flashes of mathematical pattern started appearing on the console screen, disappearing too fast to see exactly what they were. I concentrated, letting myself merge with the software running on the laptop and spreading out through the network. Now I could examine those images as they flashed up, freezing them in microseconds and letting the longer timescales of the human brain absorb them – yes, they were what I'd expected. I could feel the evil pulsing out from the central processors, more and more powerfully. I'd have to strike at just the right time, a fraction of a second before it struck me, as it had the previous four victims.

The whole screen of the console was now flashing periodically with images and not just the relatively benign mathematical ones. The speed was almost subliminal but each image lingered for just long enough for me to see what it was. It's as well I'm familiar with the sort of revolting and degrading stuff that these evil forces relish and wallow in. Frankly, they were too awful to describe, many involved myself. The most benign of them simply showed my naked body, ripped open at the heart, blood spurting out... In my line of business you learn to switch your emotions off. I was functioning at the purely analytical, intellectual and mathematical level now, woman and machine and software working as one. The lurid imagery was simply noted as a fact, as was the approaching crescendo of evil.

The screen suddenly turned black – then zoomed out to show a familiar image but coloured and zoned in such a way as no human had ever devised, every pixel radiating revulsion and evil. All the screens on connected computers in the building would be showing the same picture.... the image started sliding off the screen to the right, twisting and writhing in an incredibly hypnotic way – I watched, fascinated, my eyes fixed to the screen, my head starting to fall forward...

My laptop beeped, loudly – I snapped out of my reverie – horror, I'd nearly gone into a trance, NOW was the time to act. With all my concentration, energy, willpower, everything I had, I cried aloud to the great God to give me power and strength. Straight into my own brain I dragged my software off the network. I didn't need to look at the screens, my own eyes were displaying the images as in a virtual reality headset – now I could see a great spike, twisted barbs reddened and hanging in gore, I could feel a growing pain in my chest...

'BEGONE IN THE NAME OF JESUS CHRIST AND PERISH IN THE OUTER DARKNESS,' I yelled, at the same time launching the full power of my exorcism software into the network.

A terrible scream rent the computer room – was it me? Everything I'd ever seen or done was whirling through my brain, my eyes a kaleidoscope of colour. I'd have to black out for a few seconds or risk a dangerous overload.

'I'LL SURVIVE, EVEN IF IT KILLS ME,' I shouted and let go into the welcoming darkness...

A few seconds, or a few minutes later, I know not which, I opened my eyes. The evil had gone. I was soaking in sweat and felt like a limp rag. The computer screen was blank – then dissolved into – what – I burst out laughing, weakly. The screensaver had come up and flying toasters were flapping harmlessly across the monitor to the tinny jingle of the 'flying toaster' song.

I'd won.

I phoned Tony and asked him to meet me at the main door with a mug of strong tea.

A good sleep worked wonders and the next day I convened a debriefing session.

'They'll be no more deaths, no more problems. But this was one of the nastiest cases I've ever had to deal with on my own. You should have called me in much sooner – I could have done with some outside help.'

'What did you do?'

'Let me explain. This may sound crazy to you but its true. Remember that 4.669 was the ratio of the times between the deaths. This is a number known to mathematicians as the Feigenbaum number. It's related to fractals and occurs all over the place in nature, basically a pattern often repeats itself, ever smaller, at the ratio of 1/4.669 and this repetition goes on for ever. So when I saw that number occurring here, I became suspicious. It was the last word of the graphics artist and the nature of the weapon that really got me worried though.'

'She simply said she'd seen a man – but it didn't make sense as nobody could have escaped without being seen – and the weapon had vanished too.'

'She didn't say she'd seen a man. She died saying 'Man...' She was a graphics artist, familiar with fractal imagery. She died saying, 'Mandelbrot.' And the 'weapon' that killed her was the Mandelbrot set itself – or rather the spiked end of it, as the real part of Z approaches the value –2.'

'You've lost us now I'm afraid...'

'OK. The Mandelbrot set is a bit of simple mathematics which produces an incredibly complex image on a computer screen. Part of the image is a long spike with barb-like projections off it – look, here's a picture of it.'*

'But mathematics never killed anyone!'

'Perhaps not on its own. But some evil power entered the computer system at the Millennium, possibly exploiting a weakness created by the more mundane Millennium bugs, and then replicated itself in some way at times related to the Feigenbaum number; after 466.9 days, then 100 days, and so on. The human brain is in some ways like a computer. This force had found a way of jumping into a brain at these times and using the brain's control over the body to rip out the chest cavity as if pierced by the spike of the Mandelbrot set. The last thing those who died saw was a lurid image of the set – I know, I saw it myself.'

'And if you'd not dealt with it?'

'I shudder to think. Perhaps we'd all have seen it by now.'

* See the back cover of this book.

Jonah2

There aren't any whales at 30,000 feet above Greenland.

It's rare for Don to contact me first, but when the phone rang at three in the morning I had an inkling it might be him. He's not one to worry about a little thing like the seven-hour time difference between the North of Scotland and the West coast of America.

'Hi Lynne,' came his familiar voice down the phone, 'How are you?'

'Three-quarters asleep and in the nude,' I replied.

'Oh, sorry,' said Don, 'I thought you'd be seven hours ahead of me.'

Just like a brilliant computer scientist to forget which way the earth rotates, I thought.

'Anyway,' I replied sleepily, 'what can I do for you?'

'Do you think you could come over?' asked Don, 'I've got a problem and need your help.'

'YOU need MY help?' I asked in surprise.

'Put it like this. There's plenty of money in it if we can solve this one. Put it another way, things could turn out rather nasty if we can't.'

'What's the problem then?' I asked, being one who likes to get straight to the point.

'I'm afraid its too sensitive to talk about over the phone – but its related to the safety of nuclear weapons so it's pretty important. Could you get to Detroit for the weekend?'

'Sure could,' I replied, 'sounds interesting!'

Later that morning I booked a flight from London to Detroit for the following day. I phoned up Don and he agreed to meet me at the airport.

I'd made sure I was booked on a good old 747. Being a specialist on computer problems I've never much trusted the fly-by-wire planes, especially some of the models with only two engines. It was with some concern therefore that I discovered, on boarding my flight, that there'd been a last minute change and, lo and behold, I was on a 777. Well, I thought, hundreds of thousands of people cross the Atlantic each year on these and there's never been an accident yet – they must be pretty safe.

I'd booked a standard economy seat but alas hadn't managed to get a window; I love staring out at the clouds and watching the landscape far below. Instead I was in the middle of a row of five seats with people on either side.

Even though each seat had its own TV and video selection I wasn't tempted, much preferring to read a book. This time however I couldn't settle into the story. Something about that plane made me feel uneasy.

You know how you feel when you're just starting to come down with flu, or when you get the first signs of the visual disturbance that heralds a migraine attack. You try and convince yourself that nothing is wrong, that you're in perfect health, that your plans for the next few hours or days are not going to be disrupted. But the symptoms gradually grow stronger, till eventually you can kid yourself no longer and have to accept that you're in for a miserable time. It was like that. As time passed I became more and more sure that something was wrong with that plane and that, worst of all, it was connected with me.

A few hours into the flight I made an excuse to get up so that I could look out of the window. We were just passing the southern tip of Greenland, most of the landscape was cloud-covered but below could be seen a brown coastal landscape rising into snow-streaked mountains. It's a place I'd always wanted to visit.

Suddenly the plane banked, steeply. I could see we were turning sharply, the Greenland coast was right under the window. Then we straightened out again. I crossed the plane to look out of the other window – yes, we seemed now to be flying north along the Greenland coast.

It was when the captain announced some meaningless (to me) coded message over the tannoy and all the cabin crew disappeared up front that my heart sank and I knew that something was wrong.

A few wiggles and bumps followed in the next ten minutes but the plane continued flying north. The cabin crew reappeared with fixed looking smiles. None of the other passengers appeared concerned.

I approached one of the stewards. 'Excuse me, I'm Lynne Thomas, specialist computer consultant. You've got a problem?'

'There's no need to worry, if you would please return to your seat, we'll shortly be serving lunch.'

'You HAVE a problem. Would you kindly tell me why we're flying north, not west?'

'I'm sorry, I wouldn't know. If you would please return to your seat.'

'Look, I'm a specialist computer consultant. If you've got "fly by wire" problems I may be able to help.'

He looked less sure of himself now.

'I'll have a word with the captain. Please return to your seat in the meantime.'

Five minutes later the steward returned and ushered me up to the flight deck. I made sure to take my laptop computer with me. I'd never been into the cockpit of one of these big jets but the computerisation made it less unfamiliar than I'd expected.

'As you've gathered,' said the captain, 'we have a problem. The plane seems to be flying itself and nothing we can do at the controls has any effect. We thought it might be a temporary electrical glitch or ionospheric storm but it isn't. I've never seen anything like this before. I believe you have experience of 777 control systems?'

'Well, not exactly,' I replied, 'my speciality is in dealing with a particular kind of problem which can occur in any computer system. It might be to blame here; if I could do one or two quick tests I could find out for certain. Is there a socket where I could connect my laptop?'

I already had some idea of what to expect when I plugged in my computer.

In scrawly handwriting, across the screen, appeared the following message.

'Dear, DEAR Lynne. So sorry you're on this plane. If you try and interfere with us we'll have to crash it. Sorry there's no room for you. If you get off we'll give control back to the pilots. If you don't, we'll just keep flying north till we run out of fuel over the North Pole. Happy jumping!'

'Ever read the story of Jonah?' I asked the captain.

'Sorry, I don't follow. What's that got to do with things?'

'Look,' I said, showing him the message on the laptop. 'I'm a specialist consultant who's been called in to help out with a problem in the States. I don't yet know what it is, but it's something very serious and connected with weapon systems. Something is trying to stop me from getting there.'

'You mean someone? You mean we've got hijackers on board?'

It's no good trying to explain what I really do to these technical people, they just won't accept it. If I called myself 'computer ghost-buster' or something similar I'd be lumped in with the crystal pyramid and UFO brigade. It is however deadly serious when some evil influence starts taking over computer systems and my speciality is in dealing with such cases.

'OK, call them hijackers if you like, but not people on this plane. There's nothing I can do, they have control of your computer systems and if I try to clear them off they will crash the plane. The only thing you can do to save the lives of everyone on board is to put me off the plane.'

'What do you mean put you off the plane? We can't land!'

'I mean put me off. Throw me off, if you like. Now!'

'What? You're mad!'

I know how Jonah felt. Remember the old Bible story? Jonah was running away from God and boarded a ship to take him in the opposite direction to where God wanted him to go. God caused a great storm to arise, getting fiercer and fiercer, and Jonah had to convince the crew that he was to blame and that the only way they could save the ship would be by throwing him overboard. They were most reluctant to do this because they knew he would be drowned but he eventually persuaded them. Immediately he'd been thrown overboard the storm ceased. God then sent a whale to save Jonah's life by swallowing him and delivering him back to dry land.

There aren't any whales at 30,000 feet above Greenland.

'Look,' I said. 'Give me a parachute, survival suit, radio beacon. Notify the emergency services. All of us will die otherwise.'

'We can't do that. Its minus 50 out there. We're flying at 500mph. The shock will kill you.'

'I'm pretty tough. I'll survive. How much longer can you fly north before you're out of range of an airfield?'

'We'll be in range of Iceland for perhaps another couple of hours, after that we'll have had it.'

'That gives you about an hour to make your mind up then,' I said. 'It's a bit risky but perhaps I can convince you...' I clicked the mouse to open my 'exorcism' suite of codes and selected the mildest mode. 'I'm just going to try, very gently, to clear your system of the influence that's taken it over. We'll see what happens.'

I clicked the mouse again...

We were thrown forward as the plane plunged into a dive, engines screaming. At least, everyone else was. I'd been holding on tight, expecting such. I quickly quit the program. The plane levelled up.

On the screen of my laptop appeared the sort of vile abuse that I've seen many a time, with dire warnings as to what would happen if I tried such a thing again.

As you can imagine a certain amount of chaos and panic had

been caused among the passengers. The captain found the tannoy and apologised for the severe clear air turbulence. I showed him the screen of my laptop. 'I'm sorry,' I said. 'You'll just have to put me off the plane. Don't worry, I've always wanted to visit Greenland.'

Twenty minutes later I was as ready as I would ever be.

'We've done what we can,' said the captain. 'We've alerted the military, the jets and helicopters have been scrambled. You should be rescued in a couple of hours – if you survive. God help us if this is just an elaborate hoax.'

'It's not,' I replied, 'and I'm sure He will. Just make sure that those rescue helicopters aren't fly-by-wire!'

Equipped with oxygen mask, thermal suit, parachute and goggles I was led into the unpressurised cargo bay. I'll never forget how cold and bleak it was. It was going to be tough but I was determined. I'd survive, even if it killed me...

I was shown how to open the emergency door. It would close automatically. I'd be instantly sucked out, backwards. I turned the airlock valve...

I remember a great roar and an unbelievably cold blast of air. I must have blacked out for several minutes and came to, drifting gently downwards through a calm white mist. Of course, no wind, it was carrying me with it. How calm and peaceful. But COLD. My radio beacon – it was on. It took a few seconds to realise I was below the cloud; I was over the icecap, just an unbroken sea of white. It was impossible to tell how high up I was and only at the last minute did I see the snow coming up to meet me. I remembered what I'd been told, let the knees give way, roll onto the shoulder, disengage the parachute immediately or risk being dragged by the wind across the ice. Everything happened fast as I hit the ground. Just ten seconds later I picked myself up, no broken bones, a keen, bitter wind of perhaps 30mph blowing the spindrift across the surface of the glacier, a milky haze in the air. Now to await rescue!

To cut a long story short, I eventually arrived in Detroit two days later via Thule, some over-thorough debriefing sessions and a checkup in a military hospital. The plane, I gathered, had behaved entirely normally after I'd been thrown off. All 777s had been recalled for inspection. I knew that there was nothing they'd find.

The TV and papers made much of the story on the lines that some terrorist group trying to kill me had managed to override the control systems. I was something of a hero. 'Blonde bombshell bails out to save plane.' That sort of thing. Blonde I might be but no bombshell. Well, I suppose a bit of free advertising does no harm but neither would dying my hair brown for a few weeks while I started investigating the nuclear weapons safety problem.

'The trouble with my job,' I told Don as he navigated his way out of Detroit airport onto the Ann Arbor freeway, 'is that I can't trust anything with a computer in it.'

'Neither can I,' replied Don, 'but people like us are at least aware of what can go wrong!'

'That's fine,' I agreed, 'but how many times have computers actually tried to kill you? If I hadn't been very fit I wouldn't have survived bailing out at 30,000 feet. There's more evil than ever getting into computer systems and if it knows I'm around it'll do its best to get me, even if it means killing everyone else on a plane at the same time.'

'There's a word for that sort of thing,' said Don, smiling. 'Paranoia.'

'OK. How do YOU explain what happened then?'

'Quite simple. One of the other passengers had hacked into the control systems. Probably the whole thing was set up beforehand with the help of an insider in the ground crew. Just an elaborate bluff. If you'd stayed on the flight, he or she would had to relinquish control of the plane in the end, unless of course it was a suicide mission.'

'Hmm, I suppose you could be right this time. But there was definitely evil involved, I could sense it from the minute the plane took off.'

'People can be very evil,' replied Don.

'Changing the subject,' I said, 'why Ann Arbor?'

'It's as good a smokescreen as any. I'm doing a lecture course on computer viruses at the University Computing Department in a week's time. I've booked us accommodation on the campus. Quite normal that a visiting lecturer would like to spend a few days in the town with his partner beforehand.'

'PARTNER?'

'Just part of the smokescreen. Don't worry. I've booked separate single apartments.'

We get on well together but our relationship is purely platonic.

'OK. So what's your problem?'

'If you don't mind I'll tell you later. I don't trust the security of these hire cars. All computerised engines of course...'

The first thing I needed was a really good sleep. The next morning I freshened up with a long jog along the Huron river and round the Arboretum; it was late September and the hickories and maples were tinged with the first hints of Autumn colour. Later I met up with Don in his apartment.

'I've run a thorough test against bugs; only found one, hidden in the light-switch. If we sit behind this wire mesh and I switch on the radio-jamming that will make doubly sure.'

'What on earth is so secret?' I asked. 'Surely anyone who is that keen to know will know already!'

'That may be so,' replied Don, 'but I don't want our plan of attack divulged. Two weeks ago, the world came within a whisker of nuclear holocaust. Over a dozen, fully armed intercontinental ballistic missiles were fired off from the USA against Russia, on a Sunday morning, just before seven Michigan time. Nobody had authorised the firing. The computer systems concerned are the most secure in the world. It was minutes before anyone fully realised what had happened and at that time on a Sunday morning everyone was asleep. It was barely in time that jets were scrambled in Europe; even then it was only because the missiles were fortunately following their known, pre-programmed trajectories that they could be intercepted and destroyed. It was a very, very near thing that none got through. Plutonium was scattered across a wide area of eastern Europe and Russia. The diplomatic lines have been, as you might understand, red hot. Somehow the incident's been kept out of the public domain but it's bound to leak out sooner or later. All missile systems were placed under manual control for a short time but that in itself is very risky so a degree of computer control has now been reinstated.

'I was called in to help,' continued Don. 'I'm confident that nobody but me could hack into the computer systems. On close investigation I found spurious processes running, deep down in the operating system of some key machines. I managed to clear them using my specialist software but the next day they were back, even on isolated and shielded machines. There haven't been any symptoms of malfunction other than the spurious missile firings. It is, I think, your kind of problem and I was given permission from POTUS to bring you in.'

'POTUS?' I asked.

'Sorry. It's an acronym used a lot in government circles. Short for President Of The United States.'

'Well... You can't get much more high powered than that. So it's pretty important...'

'You might say that, yes. Oh, and he knows everything about your little mishap on the flight across.'

I didn't like the sound of it. It was a whole control system, not just a few computers.

That afternoon, in the sticky late-September sunshine, Don drove me out of town to an area of woodland owned by the University. We walked up shady paths through the trees, the crickets chirruping and the occasional humming-bird whirring out of sight in the upper branches. Red squirrels scuttled up hickory trunks. I was surprised when we rounded a corner to see a large radio-telescope dish on a building with a smooth green lawn in front.

'This used to be an optical astronomy site until the glare from the city became too bright. Now it's used by the University for radio observations.'

We walked up to the main building and, to my surprise, Don pushed a security pass into a slot and typed a few numbers on a keypad by the door. The door swung open. Don carefully closed the door behind him, we walked down a corridor and in through another door marked: 'Control Room'.

'Hi Don,' said a young man in shirtsleeves sitting at a control panel, 'you've brought your partner today then?'

'That's right,' replied Don, 'special orders of the President. Can you let us in please?'

The man looked doubtful now.

'Sorry, I'm afraid that I'm really not allowed to let her in without security clearance...'

'I was serious,' said Don. He took a paper out of his wallet and showed it to the man at the desk.

The man whistled slowly and looked at me. 'Sorr-Y madam. We just have to be careful you know.'

He pressed a sequence of buttons on the control panel then walked across to a wall display board showing a picture of some distant radio galaxy. He did something and the board opened out towards us, revealing a doorway and a brightly lit corridor. We went through and the door closed behind.

'This is the secret missile nerve centre for Michigan and the North West,' said Don. 'One more door and we're in.'

After walking perhaps 100 yards down the corridor we came to another turnstile with card-reader and keypad. Don pressed a button and spoke into a recess in the wall, presumably with hidden microphone. 'Hello, Don Paxton here with Lynne Thomas. Can you let us in please.'

He looked up at a video camera which I hadn't noticed before, and smiled.

There was a 'clunk' and Don gestured me through the turnstile. Another 'clunk' and he followed.

We walked into a large, circular control room, the walls lined with desks, computer screens and instruments and with a big horse-shoe desk at the centre of the room. Video cameras and monitors hung from the ceiling. No sooner had I entered than I was struck by that familiar feeling of unease. Don was right. It was my kind of problem.

I was shown how the missiles were controlled and the procedures for launching. It was explained to me how it happened that the team manning the centre, that Sunday morning, had no inkling from any of the instruments or computers that missiles had been fired until the phone rang. All systems seemed to be working perfectly and indicated that the missiles were safely in their silos. It was only by actually carrying out a dummy firing that they had convinced themselves that the silos were empty.

The entire computer and control system had been meticulously checked, double checked, treble checked. Nothing was found except for those spurious processes deep in the system which Don had discovered.

'What's the history of this place?' I asked.

'Built in the late fifties, upgraded several times since, completely refurbished with new equipment a couple of years ago.'

'Know anything about the site before this place was built?' I asked.

'No, sorry, before my time!'

I was glad to get out, the atmosphere seemed to be getting increasingly oppressive.

'Don,' I said, as we walked back through the woods, 'you know me. I must know the history of the site – any old Indian or slave associations, any battles, massacres, anything of that sort.'

'I've not heard of anything, but we can check in the museum. These woods were...' He interrupted his sentence as we rounded the corner to see a closely entwined couple sitting in the middle of the path. I noticed the girl, who was facing me, quickly pulling a top over her bare breasts.

'I don't know,' sighed Don, 'right in the middle of the trail...' There was nothing we could do but walk right past them, she was sitting on his thighs with her legs stretched out behind his back. The man, who was tall with a totally bald head, just looked embarrassed.

'Hi,' said the girl, smiling – then I noticed a sudden hardness of her features, a glitter in her eyes.

'Who was that?' I asked, after we'd passed.

'No idea, never seen them before as far as I know.'

'Well,' I said, 'whoever the girl was, she seemed to recognise me.'

I'd dropped asleep in the car on the way back, still a bit jet-lagged and not used to the heat, when Don woke me.

'Lynne, the cruise control has jammed!'

Even in my half-asleep state I knew what had happened. Fortunately we were still in the middle of the freeway where we could avoid accelerating or braking.

'Don't worry,' I said, 'but you'll find the brakes don't work either. I'm getting a bit fed up with this.' Which indeed I was.

Such things are however easy to deal with as there's very little in a car computer system for any evil force to get hold of. I let myself flow down into the car's electronics. 'Just get out you stupid imp and leave me in peace, will you,' I mouthed angrily and the engine suddenly revved as Don's frantic pumping of the accelerator engaged the throttle again.

'That's funny, seems to have cleared,' he said.

'It won't happen again,' I replied, 'now let me go back to sleep!'

I headed for the museums the next day but couldn't find anything particularly sinister about the history of the missile site. There seemed little I could do except go back into the control centre and try and clear the problem, blind. We made an appointment for the following day.

Overnight thunderstorms had cleared the air and it was cool and fresh when we walked into the control room. Once into the nerve centre I set to work. All missile systems had been temporarily placed under complete manual control while I worked, to be on the safe side... and there was nothing wrong. You know how frustrating it is when you take your car into the garage to find that the fault immediately disappears when the mechanic gets to look at it. So it was now. The system was as clean as a whistle, there were no spurious processes, there was nothing I could do.

I'd allowed a fortnight in the States and Don suggested we take a few days off camping in the north of the Lower Peninsula before trying once again to bottom the problem. It might shake off anyone who was watching us and perhaps, if we left the area, something would develop in the next day or two. It was risky, but it was clear that as long as I stayed around Ann Arbor, nothing would happen. We obtained permission 'from a very high level' provided we remained in contact with mobile phones and portable satellite-dish Internet link. For me, accustomed to back-packing across the rain-swept Scottish Highlands, this would be luxury camping, with a hired car and a couple of tents on the official camp-grounds. I wandered downtown and picked up a new 'Proton' for the rest of the week, we loaded up tents, bought food in the supermarket and set off for the Manistee River.

Why the Manistee? Don knew a good federal campsite where there were lots of trails through the woods which would be very attractive now the Fall was coming on. We drove a round-about route out of town before heading north on the freeway towards Mackinac and a few hours later were bumping along the dirt road to the campsite. Only one or two other tents were there; this was out-of season, after the summer and before the best colours of the fall.

It was certainly good to relax the next day, just walking for miles and miles along the trails through the hickory woods above the Manistee river. The late September sun was still hot although there had been a frost the night before. The last couple of miles back to the campsite were along the dusty yellow dirt roads which bordered what was obviously some very private property. Almost every tree had a notice nailed to it. 'Private Property. Keep Out. Trespassers will be Shot.' Don explained that some extreme right-wing sects had taken up residence in North Michigan...

A big four-wheel drive pickup was coming towards us, fast. We stepped aside to let it pass but it didn't slow at all, roaring by in a cloud of dust which enveloped us both. The driver looked familiar.

'Don,' I said, 'I think we've been recognised. I'm sure that was the girl we saw with the bald man near the missile control centre.'

'I doubt it,' said Don, 'it'll just be a Michigan face you're not used to seeing; when you see two different people with similar features you think they're the same person.'

It was another fine evening at the campsite, we lit a fire and retired to tents under a frosty, starry sky. Yet I was feeling uneasy, there was something in the air. The weather was more unsettled in the morning, the wind was rising and there was cloud about. We started out on another trail circuit but I was feeling increasingly unhappy. I took my laptop and collapsible satellite dish with me, as usual. We must have been at the remotest part of the trail, several miles from the nearest road, when Don's mobile phone rang.

'Mobile phones should be banned!' he groaned, before answering it. 'Don Paxton here.'

'Steve Foster, Michigan Missile Control Centre. We have an emergency. How soon can you get here?'

'I'm in the middle of a north Michigan forest at the moment. You could send a helicopter but it would be at least an hour.'

'DAMN! Do you know where Ms Thomas is then, she might be our last chance.'

'She's with me right now.'

'JESUS CHRIST! So you're with your girlfriend in the middle of a wood in North Michigan while we've got missiles launching and can't do a thing about it!'

'Hang on,' I said, 'give me the phone.'

'Lynne Thomas here. What's happening?'

'Neither manual nor computer missile control systems are responding. It looks like the entire American ground based nuclear missile force is preparing itself for action and we can't stop it!'

The scene was utterly peaceful. Sunbeams slanted downwards through the yellowing hickory leaves onto the path. Below, the blue of the Manistee River could be glimpsed between the trees. Nuclear Armageddon was minutes away.

'Don,' I said. 'I expect we've been watched. But I can try and work by satellite link over the Internet.'

I ripped open my rucksack, unfurled an aluminium dish and tripod and in a few seconds had my laptop and mobile phone connected up to the Ann Arbor university mainframe.

It was as I'd feared.

A concentrated beam of hate pulsed onto my screen, the usual kind of stuff, devil faces leering out of mushroom clouds, my own body bloated and peeling from radiation burns. I could fight and overcome the evil by my normal methods but it would take too long. There was nothing for it but to type in the emergency command words which I keep in reserve for desperate situations but have rarely had to use.

The screen went calm and blank.

'Sorry Don,' I said, 'your university will need a new computer.'

Don shrugged. 'What's 50 million dollars against nuclear war?'

I'd have to get through another way. 'Give me a password for the missile control system. Fast!'

'Haven't got one I'm afraid, but I do know how to hack in!'

Seconds later I was online to the main control computer and the lurid hate messages were back on my screen. Somehow I had to get past them to the missile systems.

'Don, how long have we got?'

He spoke into the phone. 'Two minutes at most. All silo doors are open and missiles are preparing for launch.'

There was not enough time. It would take hours to get through to all the systems concerned. In desperation I tried the emergency commands again.

'Our computer's blown up!' came the disembodied voice from the phone, 'but looks like the missiles are still preparing to go!'

Never have I felt so helpless. We'd been well and truly caught out. My only hope now was another Internet node, fast, never mind that it was across the Atlantic, I logged onto my home site at the Strathy telecottage where at least there was plenty of computer power and absolutely no evil influence. There was one, desperate, last chance.

'Norman HELP!' I typed down the line.

'Hi Lynne, what can I do for you,' came back the agonisingly slow reply. Thank God he was on the machine, even if typing with two fingers as usual.

I can type 120 words a minute if I have to.

'Nuclear Armageddon in 60 seconds unless... you MUST spawn these processes across the WHOLE Internet in the USA. EVERY MACHINE. NOW!'

People were running towards us along the trail. I heard shots. I just managed to type in the vital emergency words and press 'SEND' before diving to the ground. A second later my computer was smashed against a tree and somebody heavy leapt on me and held me down.

The fate of the world rested in Norman's hands.

'Strange thing to want,' thought Norman as he sipped a cup of tea while, in through the open window, drifted the sound of bees buzzing on the Autumn mombretia and the bleating of a flock of north country Cheviot sheep being slowly herded up the road. 'But I'd better do what she says.'

It took him ten seconds to clip my commands into a bit of virus code and fire it off. Ten seconds later he realised that he'd forgotten to restrict the code to the USA and sent out a second bit of coding to protect the local Caithness machines from whatever my commands would do...

Norman's virus was quite simple, it copied itself from one machine to every other networked computer and then ran my commands. In less than a minute there would be no linked computer on the entire world Internet without my emergency programme running on it; if there was anything remotely evil on that machine, even simple pornography or the nastier computer games, it would be violently destroyed. This might be computer Armageddon, but was the only hope of averting the real thing.

My assailant, then Don's, let out agonised screams. They rolled over, unconscious or dead. Silence descended. The phones, too had gone dead. A humming bird whirred in a distant tree and crickets chirruped in the sunshine. A few minutes later there was still no roar of missiles across the peaceful, clear sky.

I recognised the bald man and the girl amongst four prone bodies. They were all dead, a small hole in the back of their necks oozing a little blood.

'Computer chip implants to the brain,' said Don. 'Direct link to the Internet.'

We walked back to the campsite, there was little point in hurrying. Either the world was coming to an end or it wasn't. Fortunately the car radio was still working. Most stations were off the air. We found an emergency forces broadcast. No missiles had been launched. Many computer systems across the world had self-destructed and most countries faced months of chaos and disruption. But nuclear war had been averted. Police were seeking members of a right-wing devil-worship cult in Michigan and urgently wanted to speak to a Ms Lynne Thomas, believed to be camping with her partner in the Manistee area...

Julia 101

When the aliens came they didn't negotiate. Nor did they invade. No friendly 'Take me to your leader.' No attempt to take over, conquer. These are, after all, human ideas.

The aliens, two of the them, alighted on the planet Earth in much the way as wild geese might settle onto a stubble field in the Autumn. And they began to feed.

It didn't take long for frantic governments to ascertain that the pair had no interest in, perhaps even no understanding of, communication with people. Human life, indeed any other form of life, was simply an irrelevance to them, very likely not even noticed. Whether they were highly intelligent or merely a species of interstellar pigeon was impossible to know. Their effects, however, were utterly devastating.

Initial reports of some strange and catastrophic phenomena had come in from the central and most arid regions of the Sahara. A large area had been hit by some severe storm which had killed, indeed totally obliterated a party of nomads and had flattened several square miles of dunes. Scientists, flown in to investigate, were baffled as to what had happened. Traces of radiation were found and for hundreds of miles around there had been intense interference on all radio and TV communication channels for about 15 minutes. The few observers nearby reported a bright glow. Israel and its Arab neighbours accused each other of testing new weapons, denials were vehement on both sides.

Then a small town in the middle of the Lower Michigan peninsula, USA, vanished. Phone lines had suddenly been cut. Drivers reported a sudden opacity ahead, a brilliantly glowing white curtain across the road. Those who drove into it were never seen again. All communications on all wavelengths for miles around were drowned in static.

After a few minutes the static, the glowing curtains, vanished as suddenly as they'd come. A roughly circular area about three miles in diameter, had been flattened. Squashed would be a better description. Everything above bedrock level – soil, trees, houses, people, had been compressed into a dense clay.

Suspicions centred on Iraq, with the Chinese a close second. Again, traces of radiation, which soon turned out to be neutron activation products, heightened suspicion. There was however no sign of fission products, no evidence of a nuclear explosion.

Both China and Iraq, realising that the USA wasn't just making up the story and well aware of their danger, were outspoken in their denials and issued unusually open invitations to come and inspect military facilities. Soon, though, it became apparent that neither they, nor any human agency was to blame.

At random intervals, sometimes just a few minutes apart, sometimes after several days, somewhere on Earth, the same devastating event was occurring. There was no pattern other than that always at least a few people were killed. It was only a matter of time before a large city was struck.

Meanwhile, scientists were frantically gathering information. Satellite pictures. Overflying at high altitude. Monitoring of radiation emissions. Top multidisciplinary teams were assembled, dispersed to all the main national laboratories throughout the world and an emergency conference convened via the telecommunication network and the Internet. The conference was addressed jointly by the leaders of the USA, Russia, France, UK and China.

Just hours before, the news had come through that Albuquerque had been hit, only 100 miles from the main US National Lab of Los Alamos. A great circular area of city, taking in the university, the airport and the whole of the central business section had been flattened from the Rio Grande to the slopes of Sandia peak. Nearly half a million people had died, probably instantly. Streets, even houses, had been cut in two. Away from the main centre, it was now clear that, as had been reported elsewhere, similar, much smaller areas had been devastated, indeed circular flattened patches of all sizes could be found in the vicinity of the main area of devastation. Some roads exhibited zigzag, twisting, branching, hairline cracks.

The president of the USA, fresh from a visit to the destroyed city, was past pandering to politics or special interests when he addressed the conference.

'The fate of mankind depends on us finding out what's happening and dealing with it. Fast. We pledge you all the resources, men, money, equipment, military that you require. We're prepared to use nuclear weapons if need be. It's up to all of you, all of us in the international community. It could be any of us, any of our great cities, next.'

'What do we know?' Steven Ellis, Professor of theoretical physics and Nobel Laureate addressed the thousands of eminent scientists and millions of journalists gathered throughout the world.

'We now consider that the best hypothesis is that we are witnessing attacks from some kind of alien being.' (That woke the journalists up!) There appear to be two of them. Strikes may be minutes or days apart, we've found no pattern. Always people are killed, but there seems to be no pattern in targeting large rather than small numbers of people. No part of the globe seems to be either specially favoured or exempt, many sparsely populated areas have escaped but that's what you'd expect statistically. We now know a lot about the characteristics of the attack. This is what one looks like from the air.'

A gasp of surprise and horror circled the globe at the speed of light. The slide showed a central, black, circle. Around it was a multicoloured fringe, red turning to white at the periphery with a crinkled edge. Long, black tentacles fringed in glowing white reached out from central blob, linking randomly spaced smaller circular copies of the central blob. Each spawned smaller tendrils and smaller circles.

'You can see that the entities, or whatever they are, appear to have a fractal nature. During the attack, which lasts just under 15 minutes, radiation of all kinds and wavelengths are emitted. The spectrum is not black-body but dies off at very long and very short wavelengths. Electromagnetic radiation from gamma through X, ultraviolet, visible, infrared, radio of all wavelengths. Also some neutron, beta, positron, and we suspect alpha, meson and all the other kinds of particle which make up matter. The gamma bursts precisely match the characteristics of the range of cosmic gamma-ray bursts which we have known about for many years as coming from all directions in space and which have proved so difficult to explain. This may be significant. We have programmed satellites to detect any attack the instant it happens. We now know that two attacks occur simultaneously on different parts of the globe. Both the beginning and end of the two attacks are exactly synchronised. We have determined that radio frequencies are preferentially beamed between the two entities. There is a non-random amplitude modulation which appears to be simple binary and looks like some form of communication. We are currently attempting to analyse this. Attempts are being made to communicate with the entities but we have as yet had no response. We understand that other nations have recently tried other, more drastic measures.'

The Russians spoke next.

'As you no doubt already know, we targeted our last attack, on Novosbirsk, just a few hours ago, with a two megaton hydrogen bomb.'

A collective gasp. Only the Russians could get away with such an approach. 'We are analysing the results but it appears that our weapon, which exploded successfully, had no effect at all on the duration of the attack or the integrity of the entity.'

'We can confirm that,' replied an American voice. 'The attack ended simultaneously with the Albuquerque attack. While still visible we could detect no change in the appearance of the entity. It appeared to be completely unaffected by the explosion. Perhaps we did some long-term damage but we are not hopeful of...'

His voice was cut off and interrupted by the chairman.

'We have just heard that two more attacks are taking place. One is in Peru and the other in China...'

The conference soon split into smaller, brainstorming groups and progress was made far faster than anyone had anticipated. A number of people in the audience had gasped at that first photo of an attack, not because it was so alien but because it was so familiar. As computer hobbyists, or the parents of hobbyist children, they immediately recognised the image of one of the infinity of Julia Sets, it could almost have come straight from the screen of an Apple Mac. But which one of the sets was it?

Every fractal enthusiast has heard of the Mandelbrot set, which plots all the complex numbers whose corresponding Julia set is connected. The simple process of taking a complex number C and a starting value Z_0, calculating $Z_1 = Z_0 \times Z_0 + C$, then repeating the process over and over again for all values of Z_0 generates the Julia set of C. Immense complexity can develop with sets that centre around a cycle of values of Z which repeat, over and over again. The number of possible sets increases fast with the periodicity of the cycle, there are only three Julia sets of period 3 but there are over 2000 period 11s , over a million period 20s and the number of period 100s would be given by a '1' followed by 30 zeros.

But now there was a clue! Julia sets come in pairs, that for +C being a mirror image of that for –C. Hence, maybe, the two entities. But what were they? Steve Ellis was speaking to the world again.

'Philosophers have often speculated on where mathematics comes from. Is it an invention of the human brain? Does it exist on its own somewhere "out there"? Ladies and gentlemen, I think we now have positive evidence that mathematics has its own reality. These attacks appear to be coming from inhabitants of some mathematical space. What are they doing? Are they exploring the material universe as we study the mathematical one? Are they just the mathematical equivalent of cows, grazing on fresh pasture, perhaps the mathematical thoughts of the human brain? We can probably never know. But now maybe we can get some idea as to how to scare them off. We must attack them mathematically! Where do we start? We have the hypothesis that they are members of the family of Julia sets. We have a hunch that if we can determine which set they belong to we may be able to elbow into their mathematical space and do to them what they are doing to us! We need better pictures. If they are high period sets we may however never find which ones, it will be forever beyond the range of our computers!'

Suddenly Mandelbrot and Julia theory became very fashionable.

London was hit. Over one million people killed. Panic. The government put out a statement that, on the best scientific advice, another attack was unlikely and people should stay put. This only increased the volume of people pouring out into the countryside. The entire UK economy at a halt. Civil Defence – what was that? Something abandoned years before to save money?

Evidence mounted. It had been easy and quick to check all Julia sets up to about period 30. None matched. If the entities really did correspond to members of the Julia set, the periodicity was higher, could be 50, 1000 or 100000. They corresponded to 'C' values that were not directly attached to the main buds of the Mandelbrot set. That meant an impossible number of calculations to find out which one. Impossible? Good engineers do that before breakfast. Especially at the Arctic Centre for Supercomputing, Fairbanks, Alaska.

Enter Joe Stevenson, parallel computing whiz kid whose main ambition in life had always been to drive the biggest and fastest computer in the world at six times its design capabilities. He'd started out at the age of nine by writing Mandelbrot and Julia set programmes, by the age of 13 he was making a fortune selling computer games to Japan but gave that up as too plain boring. Now he was quite at home teasing the last teraflop out of the

Centre's massively parallel system on the most complex and esoteric problems of quantum chromodynamics. It took him a mere half-hour over a coffee break to get the Centre's computer churning out Julia sets an order of magnitude faster than anyone else had ever done before.

It wasn't enough. At this rate, to carry out a check as far as period 100 against the aliens (whose fractal nature was now catalogued to a frightening degree of accuracy) would take thousands of years. To check all the sets would of course take an infinite amount of time.

Joe went home to think about it. A quantum computer and a sieve, that's what he needed. Most fractals could be eliminated by checking just a few data points. There was no way even he could get the Newton-Raphson algorithm running fast enough to generate the required octillion solutions each second merely to make checks up to period 100 or so possible. Cellular automata – single bits – change one and compare – somehow set up a mimic of a quantum computation in massively parallel architecture, let the quantum mechanics test, simultaneously, all the infinity of sets so that the simulated wave function collapsed on the right one. By noon the next day he had a rough and ready algorithm which worked, but was still 1000 times too slow. He needed more power, the poor little machine at Fairbanks wasn't up to the job. But if he could harness the power of all the computers in the world, parallelism on a truly massive scale, he should be able to determine the Julia set in a matter of hours. He booked a flight to Los Alamos.

The Internet was commandeered. Within 24 hours, software was in place on virtually every one of the millions of the world's interconnected computers. Slow machines were assigned the very long wavelengths, the elimination of which would cut out low period solutions. The fastest machines attacked the short wavelength, high frequency regios, ruling out vast swathes of C-space. Even the humblest 286 processor would have its part to play. The master controller, at Fairbanks, started to run the whole, complex, messy system – and it crashed. Too much variability in physical message passing times. More slack would be needed, that would slow everything down but there was little alternative.

Once again, start the master machine, allocate all the millions of machines and processors their own set of wavelengths in C-space and hope for the best.

It seemed to be working. From the quadrillions of calculations a second at Sandia lab to the chuntering kiloflops of an old BBC-B on a croft on the Isle of Hoy, the most massive computation ever undertaken by mankind ground into action.

Not a second too late. Random attacks continued, as before. Devastation and calamity on a scale that would soon be threatening the very survival of mankind.

'We have a solution!' It was the Fairbanks team, ten hours into the project.

'It's a P101 and we're sending you the coordinates of the set. We're getting the picture up on the scree....' The line went dead. Every connected computer in the world stopped, hung or crashed.

Fairbanks had been attacked. But this time it was different. There had been a huge explosion, several kilotons in size. Instead of just being flattened there was a crater, over 100 metres deep. The university and many square miles of forest had been obliterated. There had been no simultaneous attack elsewhere. Joe Stevenson was a lucky man to have stayed on at Los Alamos.

'It seems like we stung them!' That was the consensus. 'Did we get those coordinates?' The team gathered anxiously round a small Apple Mac as Joe searched the mail directories. 'Yup, we've got 'em. I'll just save them to archive on the server then have a look. All we need to do to get the second entity is to change the sign of the 'y' coordinate.' He double-clicked on the mail icon... 'Stop!!' With unusual energy for a desk-bound theoretician, Steve knocked Joe aside and pushed the the Mac off the desk so that it crashed onto the floor. 'If you get those coordinates on the screen we're dead!'

'Thanks,' said Joe. 'That was a near thing. Pity it was a Mac you smashed though, not a PC...'

'Sorry,' said Steve to the puzzled bystanders, 'let me explain. When we calculated those coordinates at Fairbanks we suddenly created a new bit of mathematical knowledge, one which hadn't existed before. We elbowed in on the mathematical world with a hard, indestructible fact – and there wasn't room anymore for the inhabitant that already lived on that spot. It tried to destroy the new knowledge but could only destroy itself. Remember how our nuclear weapons had no effect on it? Remember how, when it elbows into our world, nothing can withstand it? If we write out the central coordinates of the first entity and then, even in our minds, invert the 'y' value, then we have created a second bit of new knowledge and the second entity will destroy itself and do to us what the first did to Fairbanks. Get a PC, put it in the middle of the desert and set a programme running to put up those new coordinates on the screen after leaving enough time to get well clear. Any volunteers?'

An hour later a huge explosion rocked the old weapons testing site.

Two hours later there was bad news.

'We're still getting attacks! and there's many more of them! Looks like eight simultaneously now!'

'Are they the same? Look the same, yes, but a lot smaller, Radius affected seems to be only about 500 metres.'

Steve Ellis was in command again. On a big screen he had a picture of the P101 Julia set.

'See how the central blob with the tentacles is linked by these wavy lines to much smaller blobs with tentacles. Each smaller blob spawns smaller ones and so on, Each wavy line, if you magnify it – he pressed a key and the 100 Cray processor supercomputer immediately ran a few billion iterations – you see that each line is made up of more blobs and more lines. Fractal. Looks impossibly complex but it's actually now a simple matter to systematically calculate the coordinates of all the centres down to any scale we want. That means we can eventually render these aliens harmless. When we've destroyed the eight entities currently on the loose, we'll have perhaps 100 lethal aliens of size around 50 metres across. But we can knock those out as well. We just keep going through the fractal, successively calculating the coordinates of the smaller and smaller centres till we reduce the size of the entities down to atomic scale at which they can do no harm. But we're going to need a heck of a lot of disposable computers!'

Now the main centre coordinates were known, it didn't need much computing power to calculate others. A pocket calculator could do one at a time. The trouble was that, immediately some new coordinates were calculated, whatever had calculated them was destroyed. It was deemed quickest and easiest just to set up arrays of computers and program them remotely. 8, 70, then 800 aliens, and computers, blew up. Now the scale had been reduced to such that 10,000 computers were needed. These were requisitioned, programmed and placed in a widely spaced array in the desert. Absolutely nothing happened. Some idiot had typed an 'O' instead of a zero and, in his hurry, hadn't bothered with the usual Quality Assurance checks on coding. Meanwhile, 10,000 buildings throughout the world were flattened by the entities still on the loose whose attack was as devastating as a hundred pound bomb. How embarrassing. The programmer concerned made sure it worked the second time round...

Now there were some 50,000 entities loose on earth, each about half a centimetre across. Still as lethal to people as a bullet. An attack, while the next array of machines was being assembled, killed 50,000 people across the globe.

With the entities now down to half a millimetre in size it was possible to allow machines networked on the Internet loose on the problem. Half a million machines blew up in a spectacular way but nobody was seriously hurt. A second run, to ensure none had been missed, blew up a few more. The big manufacturers, smelling government compensation, offered free replacements to volunteers. At a size of 0.05mm the entities could now do no visible damage but were still amply big enough to destroy a computer chip. A sizable fraction of the world's PCs was sacrificed to eliminate entities down to the 0.005mm scale. AppleMac users were more circumspect about destroying their machines.

At last the size of the millions of entities was such that nothing worse than corruption of computer memory occurred when one was destroyed. The Internet swung into action with remaining machines and within hours all entities had been eliminated down to atomic scale, at which size any effects would be lost in the uncertainties of quantum mechanics. The world breathed again.

Perhaps it was no coincidence that, with millions of people now clamouring for replacement computers, Applied BioSystems Inc. released its first DNA driven machine, or that, as a major program to calculate all Julia set centres down to period 120 swung into action, the mysterious gamma ray bursts from outer space gradually died away...

Medusa 2005

I may have fought imps, demons and evil powers but I've never dared to try and alter the fabric of the universe.

Computer art can kill.

Some of the worst evil I'd encountered was related to those computer fractal images which had suddenly become very popular. Striking multi-coloured pictures of spirals and whorls, images of the Mandelbrot and Julia sets, could appear very beautiful and were surely harmless. Yes – but if you dug too deeply you started uncovering some of the raw chaos left over from the creation of the universe, if you went deeper still you risked disturbing evil which had been lurking in dark mathematical recesses since before the dawn of time.

It wasn't a problem until computers became powerful enough to start invading those remote corners of the mathematical world. My first indication that the Mandelbrot set was more than just a mathematical curiosity came when I was involved in investigating the deaths of three Durham University maths lecturers. (The 37 case. You remember it of course.) Only a few specialists working on obscure branches of number theory were, however, affected.

Then came a peculiar affair when my friend Norman found out how to influence the coming week's lottery draw simply by looking at the Mandelbrot set on a computer screen. That was hushed up. The warning bells of a deep connection between the set and physical reality were by then ringing loudly but even I hadn't grasped the full implications.

It was the dreadful Warrington case (The PC Solutions murders – remember?) that really got me worried. Some raw evil Thing had taken over the computer systems and was killing people in a particularly nasty way at increasingly frequent intervals. With very little time for preparation I had to face it head on and won, but only just. After that, I couldn't see a Mandelbrot image without shuddering.

It was, I think, more than a coincidence that the fractal images of Mandelbrot and Julia sets became fashionable after I'd defeated that particular terrible corruption of the set. Computers were by then so cheap and powerful that anyone could easily generate the things. It started with ties – then T-shirts, carpets, wall-paper, even cars... everywhere you looked you were seeing those complex multi-coloured patterns of spirals and buds and petals.

It was of course a Mr Mandelbrot who first generated the pictures that bore his name. It's text-book example of a very simple process generating great complexity and in turn needing some pretty high-powered maths to understand. Not even a brilliant mathematician like Mandelbrot foresaw that the complex set named after him would kill people and form the basis of a jackpot-winning lottery system.

Mr. Julia worked out the theory in the days before computers and never lived to see the pictures of his sets, closely related to Mandelbrot images, which now also appeared everywhere. Any integer can be used as a label for a Julia set, the bigger the number, the greater the complexity of the picture and the more possible varieties. Numbers like 240 with lots of factors are especially interesting. As I discovered, sets involving the number 666 could be dangerous, Mr Julia never imagined that academic, pure mathematics could kill people.

A mathematician by training, I took care after the Warrington case to thoroughly understand the maths behind the pictures. Next time some evil involving them appeared I'd be well prepared. Unfortunately I got the maths wrong. We all know that numerical mistakes in engineering or financial calculations can have serious consequences. Mistakes in pure, abstract maths are however surely only of interest to mathematicians? Not so, I discovered to my cost, when it comes to those wretched Mandelbrot and Julia sets!

Various companies producing fractal images had started up but most had merged together or been taken over; eventually fractal designs in the UK and latterly throughout the world were mostly emanating from one company, Mandelpic Ltd. The owner/manager, Robert Urquhart, was known as something of a recluse and had set up his headquarters in the old Abbey buildings at the southern end of Loch Ness next to Fort Augustus. Why choose such a relatively remote location? Why not, these days! High speed data links meant that a computer based business could be located anywhere and, in any case, the owner had family connections in the area going back into the distant past.

I'd disliked those Mandelbrot and Julia images ever since the Durham episode. Once Mandelpic had almost a monopoly on them I liked them even less, they set my teeth on edge and made me shiver. Everyone else seemed pleased with them though, Mr Urquhart accumulated his millions and the images became more widespread and more complex, exploring larger numbers and greater depths. I hoped Mr Urquhart was no more than an entrepreneur with a flair; the potential for wilful misuse of dangerous regions of the sets had been at the back of my mind ever since that Durham affair...

When the phone-call came from Mandelpic, asking if I'd be available for discussions with Mr Urquhart, I was only too glad to comply. Evidently he needed advice on the dangers and pitfalls of the Mandelbrots, advice I would be delighted to give. I could also nicely fit in a visit to Norman and friends from Caithness who'd invited me to join them for a weekend at Melgarve bothy, just over the Corrieyairack pass from Fort Augustus. I'd have my business discussions during the week, leave the car in the town and walk over the pass to the bothy for the weekend.

I'd lived in Caithness for a spell but had moved back to

Cumbria, a much more central location for my work which rarely involved visits beyond Glasgow. I drove north through wind and rain, typical blustery early October weather, downpours through Glencoe and Fort William but skies clearing to a fine late afternoon at Fort Augustus. Accommodation was being provided for me at the Old Abbey on the following night but I'd come early to get a look around.

I soon discovered that Mandelpic was not popular locally. The whole of the Old Abbey had been ringed with a high, alarmed security fence like a jail. The gate was manned 24 hours a day. A few local people had been employed but most of the staff were from the south, living in the abbey and not communicating much with the locals. Little of the money from the company was finding its way into the area. Unfriendly, secretive, pushy – these were the sorts of words used to describe the place. When the landlady of my B&B heard that I had business there, she clammed up and wouldn't talk to me any more about it.

'Just another business trip,' I assured myself. I get to see all kinds of companies and organisations, good and bad, the common theme being that they need my help. I wouldn't choose to work as an employee for many of them; gambling, tobacco, weapons production or just plain cut-throat business, but it is individuals within these places that call me in for help, and without my help things would be much worse. So as I drove my red Porsche up to the security gate in the high fence, I wasn't too bothered. No nuclear weapons or nerve gas here, anyway.

The guard at the gate was business-like and raised the barrier to let me through, I noticed however that he was wearing a gun – how, I wondered, did they get permission for that? I carried on down the main driveway through magnificent trees to park, under a prominent video camera, near the main entrance. Collecting my laptop I strode briskly up to the security door, a pretty standard code-operated thing with microphone and video camera. I rang the bell, spoke into the mike, 'Miss Thomas to see Mr Urquhart,' smiled breezily at the video camera and waited.

The door opened and I walked in. It shut behind me with that particular 'clunk' that denotes high security. Two burly men, in other circumstances I'd have called them 'heavies', were waiting.

'This way please.' One man walked silently in front of me, the other walked silently behind me.

I now noticed that familiar feeling of unease which I get when entering premises with a 'problem'. It didn't concern me too much; why else would anyone want to see me? That was my job, of course, to sort out such problems – for a handsome fee. And this company wasn't short of money.

I was ushered into a secretary's office and a couple of minutes later in to see Mr Urquhart himself. I was rather surprised to see a man in his fifties, dark hair, double chin, turned-down mouth. Most people in these hi-tech businesses are a lot younger than me. He sat at a huge semi-circular desk that would have done for a cabinet minister, nothing on it but two computers. The office, I noticed had no windows, no decorations, no furniture other than the desk and a spare swivel chair which the secretary had wheeled in.

'Good morning Ms. Thomas,' he began in a smooth, slightly American accent. 'So pleased you could come.'

'Pleased to meet you Mr Urquhart,' I replied, 'you know my line of business presumably.'

'I know your line of business.'

Not a normal response, that. Nevermind, press on.

'I understand you have a problem and that I may be able to help you?'

'We may be able to reach a mutual agreement, yes.'

'Perhaps you could explain your problem to me? I'll then be able to see if I can be of assistance.'

Mr Urquhart suddenly spun one of the computer monitors around on its base so that I could see it. 'Have a look at this,' he said, and clicked the mouse a couple of times.

I wasn't prepared.

Even if I'd known what was coming I'd have needed to call on all the help available to resist. Something utterly horrible, the worst I'd ever encountered, pure naked evil, supreme ugliness, leapt at me from the screen of that machine. I certainly screamed. I think I heard laughter. For a split-second my sanity hung by a thread – but the inheritance of a hundred generations, years of experience, and the ultimate power of God saved me, just. I blacked out.

I came to, lying on a bare bed in a prison cell with iron bars on the windows. A memory of what I'd just seen came to mind before I could stop it and I just managed to make it to a washbasin before being violently sick. I was weak and shaking. 'Pray,' I said to myself, 'PRAY.' And I did. I calmed down. Professionalism kicked in. I locked the shocking memory safely away. I remembered that I would survive, even if it killed me.

They hadn't handled me roughly while unconscious, I was still wearing the same smart clothes in which I'd walked into the building. My laptop, unsurprisingly, had gone. I now noticed that, apart from the bed, the cell contained just a plastic chair and table, a washbasin and a toilet. On the table was a paper plate of sandwiches and a plastic cup. A drink of water would do me good, anyway.

What was going on? I had a horrible suspicion. It had better not be that...

I let myself calm down for a couple of hours, physically and emotionally. The room would certainly be watched by video cameras, I'd do nothing suspicious. I ate the sandwiches and drank more water. Out of the corner of my eye, not looking at it directly, I studied the door – looked like a computer-controlled security lock. That was a mistake on their part, if it was. Now where was the hidden video... I lay down on the bed, closed my eyes and pretended to doze but instead put out feelers, carefully probing the room for computer links, prepared now for sudden violent attack at any time. Yes, the lock was computer controlled. There were two videos, one behind the washbasin overflow, the other in the ceiling light-fitting. Also a hidden microphone in the toilet basin. Gingerly I let a feeler flow down the connections to the video... yes they led to a PC which was networked to others in the building.

I heard the door opening and leapt up. It was Mr Urquhart with a couple of heavies.

'Congratulations,' he said. ' Nobody else would have survived what you saw. I knew you wouldn't be killed but I really didn't expect you to still be in your right mind. You're pretty tough!'

'So you tried to drive me mad. That's nice of you. What do you want with me now?'

'We just want you out of the way. Not dead, you might then cause us more trouble than alive. Don't worry, Ms Thomas, we've no wish to physically harm you.'

'What ARE you doing?'

Mr Urquhart smiled in an evil-looking way.

'You obviously liked our pretty picture. We're very grateful to you for looking at it for us – we needed an expert's opinion. We're now going to let the rest of the world enjoy it too. Meanwhile you can enjoy our hospitality here.'

'People know I'm here, they'll know I'm missing.'

'You're here till the end of the week, officially. That will be quite long enough. After that... well, we shall see, we might have some other pictures for you to enjoy by then. Make the most of the time you have. Good afternoon Ms Thomas.' He closed the door.

So that was it. Mandelpic was a rich company with lots of prime-time advertising on TV. They were going to flash that picture into millions of homes, perhaps across the world... millions would die. Maybe there was backing from some hostile state or terrorist group planning to move in and take over. He wanted me out of the way. Yes, I would have sensed something was going to happen, yes I might well have alerted the authorities and managed to stop it, yes, I would have helped them to track the source to Mandelpic. Nobody else would. With me insane, or locked up, Urquhart and friends could safely get on with their nefarious business.

They hadn't wanted to kill me. That was probably superstition but then who knows. Not even I knew what role God would have for me after my life on earth.

I'd been used as a guinea pig; if that picture had such an effect on me, it would instantly kill anybody else. I was by now almost certain that it was a another manifestation of the 666 Mandelbrot. Remember the Durham case? Three maths lecturers died who were researching number theory and looked at hugely enlarged image of a tiny bud from the Mandelbrot set labelled by the number 666 × 666 × 666. I'd found that image pretty horrible but, with my training and strength, it hadn't hurt me. Probably Mandelpic had used its huge computing power to generate a picture a level deeper, corresponding to 666 multiplied by itself four times over (666 to the power of four). Perhaps even now they were working on a still more terrible 666 to the power of five.

The Gorgon Medusa, in Greek mythology, was one of three monstrous daughters of the sea god Phorcys and his wife, Ceto, covered with golden scales and having snakes for hair. Anyone who looked at the face of the Gorgons would be turned to stone. Now the Medusa was coming alive for real but with her power increased a billionfold by televisions and computers.

Perhaps I could still manage to stop them. I could easily use my powers to generate a few simple imps which would crash the Mandelpic computers. The trouble was that they almost certainly had that picture backed up and ready to transmit. If they detected interference from me they'd probably send the picture out immediately, perhaps not to cause as much damage as might have been, but still to frightful consequences. Now if I could alter it without them knowing... If I could change it somehow, perhaps base it on 665 instead of 666, it would be harmless but appear almost identical and Mandelpic would never know until it failed to have the desired effect when broadcast.

Could I do it? With the aid of my trusty laptop I could easily have downloaded their software, changed it and send it back. Without the laptop it would be a manual job – let myself flow down the link to the PC and into the network, locate the main computer, find the source code...Yes, I could. It would be slow, hard work but possible. Any good craftsperson can work without power tools if need be!

I dozed as much as possible till two in the morning by which time only a few shift personnel would be working the computer systems. Lying still, eyes shut, I let my consciousness flow down the line from the hidden video camera to the controlling PC. Like a dog following a bad smell I followed the network node leading to the central processor of the supercomputer from where the evil emanated. I found the disc where the source code was stored. How do you alter source code without writing it? I can only describe it as like playing really difficult music; you just immerse yourself in it and it happens by sheer simultaneous concentration and relaxation. Find the central loop, put a factor 665/666 in the angle – NO of course 666 was $3 \times 6 \times 37$ – I'd have to go to $3 \times 6 \times 36$ which was 648...how to get that last 36 – remember the angles aren't measured from the true centre of the circular bud but from the coordinates which come out of solving the equations – the buds aren't quite symmetrically placed...Can't find that bit of code. How does Newton Raphson work... concentrate... Never was mathematics worked out in such strange circumstances and with such urgency.

Do a little test. It's not working. That's not a 36 bud. It's obviously different. Must be a mistake in my code...Try again. Blast – can't get the 36 buds – what's going wrong?

A couple of hours of this was as much as I could do. My brain would crash, probably by means of a stroke, if I pushed on much more. Something was WRONG. In desperation I left what I'd done, it would produce completely wrong pictures and they'd almost certainly notice...

I let my consciousness flow back up the network into my body and immediately collapsed into deep sleep.

The sound of the door opening and my breakfast being put on the table woke me. I needed the toilet and a good wash. No privacy with two video cameras watching me. Nothing I could do about it.

Would they find out? I was sure Urquhart would come and gloat.

He did. He came in mid-morning, flanked again by his heavies.

'Well well, Ms Thomas. Trying to be clever were we? Don't worry, we've disconnected the video monitors from the network so you can't try that one again. I'd really have thought someone like you would be better at maths and your computer coding was pathetic. Why anyone pays for your advice I've no idea. Anyway let me warn you that if our computers detect any more interference, then your favourite picture will be beamed straight onto any computer or television screen in all the schools in Scotland. Just as an aperitif for the main exhibition, you understand but I'm sure you wouldn't want to have all those dear little school children on your conscience, would you? I think we understand each other.'

'So,' I said. 'When's the big release?'

'Ah, that would be telling – but not long. I'd make the most of your time if I were you...'

My only hope now was a very risky plan 'B' but it would have to wait till the small hours again. If that picture was released on the Mandelpic adverts before then – well there was nothing I or anyone else could do.

The day dragged, I had plenty of time to work out where my maths of the previous night had gone wrong. And kick myself. Of course. The subsidiary buds were evenly spaced around a centre which wasn't either the centre of the main bud or the centre derived from solving the equation but further along the line joining the two. I'd known that years ago and forgotten it. Blast. Well, too late to do anything about it now. All I could do was go over my next plan of action and pray for help...

Two o' clock in the morning. Lie on the bed, pretending to sleep, but let a feeler of my consciousness slip into the door security lock. It's so easy for me to launch a wee 'imp' which disables the system and all the connected ones throughout the building. Against all the rules and not something I'd normally do but then these were extenuating circumstances. Without my help, they'd now need to install an entire new security system to recover.

Carrying my shoes in hand, I simply walk out of the now-open door into the dimly lit corridor. Which way out? Easy, just head away from that feeling of evil and discomfort emanating from the central computers, just take every turn or door which leads me away.

Nobody about.

Creep down the stairs to the main door. This one's open too. Almost too easy, this. Now I'm out in the grounds, barefoot across the gravel to make as little sound as possible. My car's gone, I didn't expect it to be still there. Weather relatively mild, a breeze in the trees, some light from a half-moon. That should help...

Put shoes on. Fortunately decent platform soles, not high heels. Walk quietly down the drive to the floodlit main gate. Yes, the security man is there, in his little booth, lights on. Looks like he's reading. Pools of darkness beyond the barrier. Now for it, quick sprint, duck under the barrier, sprint through the floodlit area. A shout – but I'm in the safety of darkness before a shot rings out. Now alarms are sounding. They'll have dogs... I've just a couple of minutes... The river – I can hear it through the trees – push through the undergrowth and into the dark, cold water. They'll expect me to go upstream, I'll go down, to the loch. Water's not too cold, fortunately, but difficult with boulders and stones in the dark.

Already I can hear dogs barking. Here's the loch – the far shore about 500 metres away, dimly visible in the half moon. Wade in. Start swimming.

I'm still dressed in my smart clothes, not designed for this sort of thing. I can swim a couple of kilometres in warm water but am no good in cold, I'm too thin. 500 metres in cold water, should just make it. I'll survive, even if it kills me. Steady breaststroke, keep the moon to my right. Flashing lights and dogs barking in the distance. Hopefully I've given them the slip. Getting cold.

Far shore seems no nearer. Hands and feet going numb. Waves small, fortunately, wind's blowing up the loch. Cold's getting me. I'll make it. I must. Shores drawing nearer, I think. Keep on keep on, Lord, give me strength...my knee bumps on a submerged boulder. I splash into the shallows. Shivering violently, teeth chattering, but still moving.

A small stream runs down the steep-hillside through the wood. Keep in the stream bed, scramble up, feet and hands completely numb. Climb fast, there should be a road up here. Oh for a map and a torch! A track. Turn south, start running, stumbling and shivering. Now the road, must risk a mile on it, but they'll not have tracked me here. Run! As fast as I can! Shoes not designed for running, clothes soaked. Can't run with a tight skirt. Stop, rip it up the sides, that's better, a bit more like running shorts. Car coming! Desperate scramble over dry-stone wall and drop other side as it sweeps past. Climb back over and start running again. Can't be far now to track. Down over bridge – must be the River Tarff – where's that track – at last, a signpost, can't read it in the dark. Turn off the road, keep running. Stumble over boulders and fall, probably cutting hands and knee. Keep going, keep going, keep going... A steep climb, at last I'm warming up. Got to stop, no breath. No sign of pursuit. It's around three in the morning. Breezy, fresh, a few spots of rain. Moon's gone behind cloud.

Ahead, 15 miles of the Corrieyairack pass. Up to 2500 feet. In the dark, the wind and the rain, in city clothes. This is the one route they'll never expect me to take. Ahead, Melgarve bothy, friends, help. Must get there before seven. Now I've escaped, Mandelpic will be transmitting that picture at the first opportunity, probably prime breakfast TV....

I'm tough, I tell myself. I'll survive. even if it kills me. But it's a long rough road ahead; I know, I've taken a mountain bike over the pass, in fine weather and daylight...

Although once a good road, the track has eroded in many places down to its bouldery foundations, erosion made worse by 4 × 4 vehicle recreational use. It's hard going in daylight, much worse in the dark, and not a place or time to be in a desperate hurry. The rain is steady now and the wind is picking up from the south-west. Already soaked from my swim across the loch I can't get any wetter but could get very cold. Women do better than men in such conditions, with that extra layer of fat, not that I've much surplus. I just hope I can generate enough heat by my exertions to keep warm; pray for strength...

After the first dip the track climbed again, under a line of pylons which also crossed the high pass. I could hear the wind howling through the wires. Already my feet were sore from those once-smart shoes which I hoped would hold together. I do a lot of running across rough country so my ankles were strong but it's tricky in the dark when you don't know how your feet will land, especially in towny footwear. Every so often I'd go flying, collecting more minor cuts and bruises but I just picked myself up and carried on...

The last two miles give a long, steady climb. I thought I'd reached this stretch but then the track dipped down again, over a bridge with a stream roaring below, before zigzagging on up. I could only walk this section, fast, the gale-driven rain now really stinging from the side; my hands and feet numb with cold, but my body warm enough – just.

The wind must have been gusting to force ten near the top, I was on hands and knees at times when not trying to shield my face and eyes from the lashing rain. Somehow I stumbled across the top and into a sheltered corrie where the track, rougher than ever, zigzagged down in the dark – total dark, black with the dense mist of thick cloud. More than once I simply lost the track and had to retreat to find it again; the track was little more than boulders with water running down in runnels. Stumbling, hurrying, getting more knocks and bruises, I'd need a day or two in hospital when this was over.

The track levels out at the base of the corrie then sweeps on down the exposed hillside in long straights. I remembered that the going was a bit easier beside the track, tried to run and fell awkwardly, twisting a knee. That's it, I thought, but the leg still walked.

I must have looked quite a state when I finally almost crawled into Melgarve. It was 6.30 in the morning and just getting light. Last time I'd been here was on a fine evening. I'd relaxed in the sunshine. Things were a bit different now.

In Tolkein's *Lord of the Rings* Gandalf, the wizard, has to face the Balrog, a new and terrible enemy. Gandalf is already exhausted but knows he must summon up strength as never before. 'A

Balrog. What an evil fortune. And I already weary...' It happens to us all in life, sooner or later. It happens to me more than most.

'And I already weary.' Many, many of my ancestors had faced the same. Weariness is not an issue. I was alive. I could think. I must fight.

Thank God, people were staying at the bothy. Somebody had heard the door open, was moving.

'Norman?' I shouted.

'Lynne – is it you?'

'Just about,' I replied, 'please, quick, get a fire lit. I need help. Fast.'

By now torches were switched on, turned on me.

'Lynne!! Are you OK? What's happened?'

'Apart from being covered in mud and bruises, dripping blood, soaking wet, shivering and exhausted I'll be fine – if you can get me some dry clothes, a mug of hot sweet tea and a computer!'

'You'd better get into a sleeping bag and warm up!'

'No time. Look this is urgent. I'm too cold to talk. Quick, get that fire lit and some tea and I'll try and explain.'

Already a Primus was roaring and water was heating. Paper and sticks were starting to crackle on the fire. Never mind modesty – as quickly as I could with my numb hands I ripped off my wet things and covered myself up with the offered layers of sweaters and trousers. I was shivering violently but was not dangerously cold. Hot tea wasn't perhaps the best idea for someone in my state but the psychological boost would do more good than the physical harm. I'd been looking forward to that mug of gloriously sweet smoky brew for the last four hours.

I sipped the nectar (seven spoons of sugar), crouched in front of the growing fire – surely still the greatest discovery of mankind! Just for a minute I felt happy, at peace. I'd made it – but this was a lot more than a tough hill expedition. The hardest part was still to come – and I already weary.

'Norman, you've got your laptop with you?'

'Of course. Where's yours?'

'Stolen I'm afraid. Anyone else got a laptop here?'

'There's an English couple staying who've driven up here, they might have one in their van but they're asleep in the next room.'

'You'll have to wake them. This is a matter of life or death. Meanwhile – can you log onto the Strathy machine – fast – and get my software downloaded...' Fortunately I had a copy of all my crucial software on the powerful Strathy setup.

'I hope the satellite link works in this glen,' said Norman, anxiously. 'Have something to eat while I'm trying. Bill! Get Lynne some of that fruitcake and get some porridge on!'

Norman knew that something serious was up, but goodness knows what the others staying in the bothy thought. This strange woman appears off the hill in a dishevelled and exhausted state, fit to be stretchered out, and demands two computers...

Meanwhile the couple in the next room had been unceremoniously woken and were wondering what on earth all the frantic activity was about. Bill, Norman's friend, had managed to persuade them that the computer was a life-or-death matter and so, still clad in long-johns and vest, the man had ventured out into the storm to retrieve a laptop from his van.

When he came back in I already had Norman's laptop glowing in front of me and was simultaneously trying to shovel fruitcake, porridge and tea into my mouth. I'd need all the strength I could get.

'Just get me the breakfast programme on ITV please but DON'T look at the screen once you've got it, please...'

'What on *earth* is going *on,*' came a posh English female voice from the next room.

'End of the world as we know it in half an hour or so. Only I can stop it!' I shouted in reply. Best to tell the truth sometimes.

'Well you could let some of us get some sleep!'

Bill knew enough about me and Norman to realise that something dire was up but could only look on in a bemused manner. What the Englishman thought I'd no idea. Perhaps he got back into the sleeping bag with his partner. Frankly I was too concerned about other things to notice.

Next job was to contact Don in Oregon. I needed his expertise to hack the Mandelpic computer, fast. I hate mobile phones but was mighty glad Bill had one. Thank God for good friends. Don wasn't the least bit worried about being woken at one o'clock in the morning, West coast time, and knew that if I wanted his help, I really wanted it. No questions asked. 'Confirm the company name and address, any idea of their URL – right, got their web-site. Just give me two minutes to get past their firewall, then link to my site and you're in!'

By now, at around 7.30, the breakfast television viewer numbers would be peaking. This is when I expected Mandelpic to act.

'We'll be back with the headlines following the break,' said the presenter...

I wasn't ready, but I'd have to try my best if the Mandelpic advert came on – please, please just normal adverts I prayed – and they were. I breathed a sigh of relief. I'd another 15 minutes to recover strength, make plans, take stock, pray.

I could, probably, block the picture going out from Mandelpic. But how could I stop them doing it again, another time, or on American TV, or on their website – their website! I'd forgotten that.

I called Don again. 'Don, can you mount an attack on the Mandelpic website, make sure it goes down as fast as possible!'

'No bother, just give me 30 seconds...'

Don is probably the world's number one expert on hacking and computer viruses. He could disable anything.

'That's the site off,' he came back a minute later, 'it'll take them at least a few hours to recover.'

I had now perhaps ten minutes before the next commercial break. Mandelpic would know they were under attack and would almost certainly transmit their picture then. But even if I managed to stop Mandelpic this time, sooner or later they or someone else would show that picture or a similar one across the world. The old Medusa was coming to life again...

Norman was one of the few who knew about the original Mandelbrot 666 problem and could understand the danger.

'The trouble is,' I explained, 'the patterns are enshrined in basic mathematics. It's part of the fabric of the universe. There's nothing we can do about it, any more than we can disable atom bombs by making uranium or plutonium non-fissile. Our technology has released the genie, or I should say the Medusa, in a really big way now.'

'Hang on,' said Norman, 'are you quite sure you can't change it?'

'No-one can change the basic logic of the universe. You can't make 1 + 1 add up to 3.'

'Wait a minute though,' replied Norman, 'has anyone ever PROVED that those particular numbers give those patterns?'

'You probably can't,' I said, 'it just happens to be so.'

'Exactly. You must know about Godel's theorem.'

'Of course. Godel shocked the mathematical world last century by showing that there's an infinite number of things in mathematics which can't be proved and just happen, by random chance, to be true.'

'Well,' said Norman, 'suppose the particular appearance of those Mandelbrot 666s is just one of those random things which happens to be true. Surely it could be altered without affecting anything else, it could just as easily have been different.'

'Only God could do that.'

'Well, perhaps with God's help, maybe you and Him together, maybe God needs YOUR help. Remember in the book of Job how God admits how hard he finds it to keep evil, in the shape of the great Leviathan, under control.'

'I'd have to be a megalomaniac to believe that I...'

'Well, perhaps you would. But I think you should try.'

'Norman. I may have fought imps, demons, evil powers but I've never dared to try and alter the fabric of the universe!'

'It may be the world's only hope.'

I said nothing. It might be. But how – surely it was hopeless – but then if I didn't try, no-one else would. And I already weary.

Five minutes to go. The bothy fire was blazing cheerfully, the rain hammering on the window, the wind roaring in the lum. I sipped a third mug of hot tea. My body felt lethargic, craving sleep, the cuts and bruises were stinging and aching. It would be so nice just to drift off. But what sort of world would I wake to?

I thought of a hundred generations in my line before me. I thought of those who'd gone to the stake. I thought of the One who'd gone to the cross. I prayed again, 'Lord, give me strength.'

The commercial break was just beginning on the breakfast TV.

My heart missed a beat. That was the Mandelpic jingle. Now was the time!

Fierce, total concentration. Forget everything else. Woman and software as one, leap across the network to the Mandelpic computer. No way in to the core – a barrier, impenetrable. 'Lord God, use your power, through me, help me!' I shouted. I could sense the data streams pouring outwards as Mandelpic began the transmission. That might give me a chink by which I could get through their protection. Metaphorically, almost physically, I charged.

Suddenly I had power, never before had I felt power like it. Not in my own strength – yes, I know all about that but this was the limitless power of God working with me, through me, in a tangible way. I charged into the evil data stream which broke before me, a blizzard of bits and bytes and numbers flying off in all directions. I charged, straight down the line down through the hurricane of flying data to the naked evil of its source. It came out to meet me. It was strong. But with the infinite power of God, acting through me nothing could stand, not even evil left over from before the dawn of time, not even primordial chaos which had never been transmuted into order at the creation. Now, some 10 billion years later, God was taming a remaining bit of formless and empty darkness over the surface of the deep.

Greater and greater power drove down, surely the evil would crumble before it, something had to give, it could be me. I felt something go. Resistance vanished suddenly, in a huge burst of energy, a huge explosion. I almost fell forward into it but managed to hang on, managed instead to divert the burst of power upwards, outwards...

I was back in the bothy. The laptop had crashed. The TV picture on the other machine had gone too. The fire was still crackling cheerfully. A minute later the building shook gently, as in a minor earthquake. Then a faint rumble, above the wind.

A huge explosion had totally destroyed the Mandelpic headquarters, leaving a crater which soon became another bay of Loch Ness. A couple of eye-witnesses spoke of a searing beam of fire shooting upwards into the clouds.

There was much damage locally, with broken windows and such-like, but nobody seriously hurt. A meteorite strike, the experts finally concluded, a chance in a billion. I was assumed dead, with everyone else from Mandelpic, till later that day I staggered into Fort Augustus dressed in my torn, tattered and soaked business suit. Norman had actually let me off a quarter of a mile away but my story was that I was out early, walking along the shore, when the place blew, had been thrown into the loch, managed to swim ashore then lapsed into unconsciousness before crawling to safety.

Two days in the Raigmore Hospital in Inverness had me well on the way to recovery. Saviours of the world don't have it easy though. I'd had no pay and the insurance company wouldn't cough up for my Porsche or even for my laptop. Meteorite strikes weren't covered.

The fashion for fractal pictures died out almost overnight. Suddenly everyone found them very boring and all much the same. The 666 problem had indeed vanished, now those bits of the set were just a few ordinary spirals. Within six months, too, the Durham mathematicians had their comprehensive theory which had eluded them for years.

The Gorgon Medusa, I remembered from my Greek mythology, could be killed. It was the other two gorgons that were immortal...

Highland Cross

Jumping off a helicopter onto a flooded, collapsing dam is not exactly my first choice of activity after running and cycling 50 miles across the Scottish Highlands.

Never leave your computer behind. You don't know when you might receive a desperate call for help or a sudden, unexpected, attack. But really. A charity run and cycle across the Scottish Highlands. What could be more innocent? What possible use could a computer be on a steep and rough 20-mile mountain run followed by 30 miles of cycling, in the company of 600 other competitors? Fortunately these days my most basic and essential software runs on a little palm-top.

I'm not one for competitive sport but keep myself fit with running and cycling and do occasionally take part in fun or charity events where I often surprise others by turning in a pretty fast time. So when my friend Norman phoned from the North of Scotland to to ask if I'd be in his team of three for the Highland Cross, it seemed like a good idea.

I'd heard vaguely of the annual midsummer event in which 600 people run and cycle from coast to coast across the Scottish Highlands, thereby raising huge sums of money for charity. Presumably it was a relay event, I could cycle while Norman and his other friend could split the running. Only on receiving my individual entry did I realise that all competitors made the full crossing comprising 20 very rough and hilly miles running and 30 miles cycling on roads. I'd need to do some serious training. Norman reckoned that his 'computer geeks' team would provide a bit of balance in a field which mostly comprised toughened and superfit Highlanders who typically worked 24-hour shifts on oil-rigs.

The Highland Cross should actually make a nice break from the normal pressures of work. As it happened I'd had a particularly unpleasant assignment in May and a few days in the Highlands, camping and concentrating on physical activity, was just what I needed.

The event is renowned as a masterpiece of organisation. Runners take rough hill paths from Morvich, on the west coast, through Glen Affric to the end of the tarred road then pick up their bikes and cycle down through Cannich to Beauly. Buses are laid on to take competitors across in the morning, large lorries take the 600 bikes up to the end of Glen Affric to be set out in rows for runners to collect. There's a comprehensive network of drink/watering stations, first aid and mountain rescue back-up, a helicopter, indeed the whole event is run like a military campaign by an organiser who is probably an ex-general. Not least is the meal laid on for all 600 finishers by volunteers at Beauly. It's always a great Highland occasion, a tough endurance test which can be pretty painful in the doing but which everybody confesses to have enjoyed in retrospect. That was until the 2004 event...why did I have to take part in THAT one? Of course I knew why. It most certainly wasn't coincidence.

Fortunately I'd no inkling of what lay ahead as I drove north on the Friday. I had a little trepidation about the hard physical endurance test, the difficulty being not so much in covering the distance, but in doing it in a reasonable time like four hours (the winner would probably manage in under three and a half) so as not to let Norman down too badly. I knew that midsummer weather in the north-west could range from hot sun to midges to cold driving rain; the rain looked more likely this time as it was cool and unsettled with a bad weather forecast and a deep Atlantic low approaching.

I'd chosen to camp for the night and would meet Norman in Beauly early the next morning when we boarded the bus for the ride over to Kintail. I knew of a good camping spot near the edge of Boblainy Forest, just beyond the end of a convenient minor road and high above Glen Convinth.

Boblainy Forest is an unusual place, perhaps 20 square miles of forestry plantations but containing remnants of ancient woodland which has stood since the end of the last glaciation. There are steep hidden valleys, old paths, ancient log bridges, remains of settlements and, deep in the heart of the forest, a secret high waterfall. In spite of the modern plantings, forest roads and recent timber extraction it's a really wild place with capercaillie, wildcats, deer, pine martens and an insect population that would rival the Amazon. Worst are the ticks which swarm up the grass-stalks in thousands – never walk through Boblainy with bare legs! It's a forest where those who aren't into maps and route-finding can get badly lost. All in all a great place with which I really empathise, it was one of the attractions of coming north for the 'Cross' to be able to pay the place another visit.

By early evening, as planned, I'd pitched the tent and eaten my meal, allowing time for a couple of hour's gentle walk into the forest to renew my acquaintance with the Cul na Skiach Falls. The forest still had the same old wild atmosphere, it seemed less friendly than I remembered but that was probably because it was years since I'd been there. The Bruaich Burn, which winds through the deep heart of the forest, was now much more open, the pines had been felled to allow native alders and birches to regrow. It was, however, just as much of a scramble through undergrowth as it had always been, in and out of the burn, to reach the hidden waterfall. Although water levels were low it was as fine as ever, a deep scoop out of the heart of the forest with a near vertical rock-face down which the stream tumbles for a hundred feet into a pile of huge boulders. All around is a tangle of thick undergrowth, the place is a miniature of the high waterfalls of Venezuela. I followed my old scrambling route up the side, hauling myself up on birch roots and branches, climbing through and over fallen trees and slithering on steep scree to the crest of the fall which gives a tremendous view out over the jungle-like forest.

For some reason I'd been feeling more and more uncomfortable as I climbed. This part of the forest was less wild than it used to be with a new forest road coming within a quarter of a mile of the top of the falls and much felling and clearing of windblown trees. Crossing the new road I picked my way through the tangled branches and stumps towards an open ride leading back into the forest. There were low walls and piles of stones ahead; I'd never noticed them before as they would have been hidden by the thick plantations. This must be the remains of the Cul na Skiach settlement, one of many from which people were driven in the 19th century to make way for sheep grazing. The sheep didn't last, being replaced by deer for hunting and latterly the forest, planted without feeling right across the old hearths and fields.

Normally there is a quiet, sad yet peaceful feel to these old clearance settlements. Not so here. I realised now from where that feeling of discomfort had been coming; there was strong sense of unfriendliness, even hate, coming from those old stones. It was almost a physical barrier through which I had to push in order to cross and reach the forest ride. Something didn't want me there. Well I wasn't staying and had no intention of investigating, it was no business of mine and whatever was so unfriendly would just have to come to terms with the world as it was. Still, it spoilt the evening and the shadow remained with me all night. I didn't sleep well and was glad to be back at the car by seven the next morning.

The car wouldn't start, a very rare event since I always drive a pretty new model and get it regularly serviced. (I never felt like replacing my Porsche after the Mandelpic episode. Perhaps I should have.) At least I was parked on top of a long hill down which I could coast, trying to bump start, but all to no avail.

There was no time to investigate the fault, I had to be in Beauly for 7.30 to get the bike loaded. This is where teamwork helps, I called up Norman on my mobile and in ten minutes he was out with a tow rope. It was a rush but we made it onto the bus just five minutes before it left.

The bus-ride across Scotland, from east to west, is one of the best things about the Highland Cross, over the pass to Drumnadrochit, the 1 in 7 hills quite a test for a fully laden old Highland omnibus, then down Loch Ness and through Glen Morriston to the mountains of Glen Shiel. A landscape of legend and history and beauty but one which the modern Highlanders on the buses just take for granted. A hubbub of conversation, recounting tales of past ' Crosses', of marathons, training, injuries, adventures...

The rain had started, only light in Beauly, but increasingly heavy as the convoy of buses made its way down Loch Ness. Everyone does their best to take in as much fluid as possible before the gruelling run and soon a toilet stop was demanded, the men lining up along the roadside...some women disappeared down the bank into the probably tick-infested grass... I'd wait till Morvich! We'd dropped behind the other buses and as we climbed the hill towards the Cluanie dam in the steadily worsening weather, the bus got slower and slower as the engine raced. Then it stopped. The clutch had burnt out.

'It's all your fault,' joked Norman, 'two breakdowns and it's not yet ten in the morning.' I didn't say anything. He could be right.

One bus always sets out early for walkers who have a two-hour start on the rest of the field. It was fortunate that just after we'd broken down, the walkers' bus came down the road from Kintail, heading back to Beauly. It simply turned round, we all decamped onto it and resumed our journey.

Glen Shiel was quite a sight, white water roaring down all the hillsides, the main river in spate, floods of water across the road, curtains of rain sweeping up the glen. It would be a very wet 'Cross'. At Morvich some must have been very tempted to stay on the bus and ride back to Beauly. People were very quiet as we walked up the road through the soaking rain towards the start. Men and women were huddling under trees and against buildings to get changed, many wore black plastic bin bags as some protection against the cold and wet. It would be even worse higher up but I'd be running fast enough to keep warm. So shorts and a light sweat-shirt it was. My palm-top, in its waterproof case, went in a little zip pocket in a very light windproof top which I could carry in my hand once I'd warmed up.

This was a rather special Highland Cross in that 100 members of the Clan MacKenzie were taking part to commemorate the historic associations the route held for them. It had been a vital drove route in the past and there had been an important victory over the Clan Mackintosh in 1604 following escalating disputes over cattle, land and reprisal murders. A large contingent, clad in tartan running gear, was much in evidence; they were planning to run and cycle in convoy. Most would not be especially athletic and would find it a big challenge just to complete the event in a target time of six and a half hours. Norman expected to take around five hours whereas Pete, the third member of our team was aiming for under four.

Shivering and miserable, 600 runners awaited the starting gun... then we were off. Within 100 yards everyone's feet and legs were soaked, the track dipped into a swollen burn and runners were forced through like sheep through a sheep dip. 'This is normally the dry section,' said someone... Already the leaders were streaking ahead, I followed as well as I could, the main bunch behind. The stony track climbed up and down, disappearing at times under big deep puddles or swollen burns, a roaring river to the left. Mountainsides streamed with water. Sheets of rain drove up the glen. Some people would get very cold.

The emergency support helicopter roared low overhead, disappearing up the valley into the haze of rain. Ahead was the first watering station with water and isotonic drinks provided, before a steep climb into the hills. I'm better on the steeps and was taking it relatively easy on this fairly level stretch, just making sure I didn't lose too much ground. I was gaining slowly on three runners, a team keeping together but taking up most of the track. Perhaps it would be best just to stay behind them. Several people were catching me up, running just behind. It was difficult to see the footing ahead as we dipped towards another stream with brown water rushing over hidden boulders, I dropped back a bit and was suddenly pushed, hard, from behind. Being pretty nimble I managed to avoid falling, somehow leapt from boulder to boulder without losing my balance, almost fell forward on the far side of the stream then regained my footing and ran on. Now I looked round. Four runners, taking up the whole track, were closing in on me. Ahead the three seemed to be slowing up. Now someone was beside me. I was being boxed in!

The track runs through rough grass, rushes and boulders, you can run beside it but it's harder going. To the left was the river, roaring in spate, with a narrow strip of ground between it and the track. On the right was a tall, fit looking runner in an unmarked T-shirt. The track in front was blocked by three more runners. Four lay behind me, also in plain T-shirts...what was happening?

I stopped. Suddenly. The runners behind hadn't expected that and were past before they, too, could stop. That gave me a chance. I sprinted as hard as I could, off to the right, leaping across a deep stream, balancing on rocks, tearing through rushes and bog to regain the track in front of the three who'd try to block my way. No way was I taking it easy now, they'd have a hard job to catch me. Why were they trying to nobble me? Surely not because...yes, I had a good chance of winning the women's race. Not many women actually take part and the fastest time was likely to be around the four hours which was my target time. I was a dark horse and may have surprised people by my speed, the leading lady was not far in front of me. I hadn't meant to try especially hard to win but if that was their game I'd show them!

I raced through the first drinks station without stopping, in this cold and wet I could miss the odd cup of water and most certainly didn't want to be caught by those men. Helpers huddled under layers of waterproofs. Someone was trying to get a radio to work without success: 'Hello, Hello, are you receiving me, hello, hello...' Round, down, over a footbridge with a roaring brown torrent below, the leading men already strung out up the steep path ahead.

A succession of steep rough climbs and short undulating sections takes runners up past another watering station, high above spectacular waterfalls, to the open glens at 1000 feet above sea-level. Being better on the climbs I jogged upwards as hard as I could, soon catching the leading woman. Cutting a corner on a steep staircase of stones I passed her and looked back, to see an expression changing from surprise to hate.

'Why you...' she yelled out, the rest of her words lost in the roar of the wind and rain, which was perhaps as well. And this was meant to be a charity fun event. Some seemed to be taking it in deadly earnest.

I grabbed a cup of water from the bedraggled helpers at the drinks station above the falls and raced on. The weather was even wilder and wetter up here, fortunately the wind was from behind; I was fit and fast enough to keep warm but there could be an exposure risk for the slower people. It must have been sheer misery for the helpers, standing for hours in such conditions. At the highest point of the route stood a man, clad in layers of clothing and waterproofs and looking as impervious as a rock to the wild elements. One of the team providing a radio link, he too seemed to be having problems with equipment; bits of wire and tape were lying around and there was no evidence that anything was working.

Low cloud blew across this highest part of the route, not even the helicopter was flying. Just for a minute or two, in the mist, there were no other runners in sight and I could have been the only person for miles. It was then that I noticed that familiar feeling of oppression. No, it couldn't be, not here, miles from any computer, in the middle of a Highland rainstorm on a fun charity run across the hills – perhaps it was just me, I'd been going flat out for over an hour and was soaked, covered in mud and peat, out of breath, bruised from a fall... But I'd check. Slowing up, still with one eye on the rough terrain in front of my feet, I unzipped my palm-top from its case. A minute in the rain should do it no great harm but it was difficult to operate while leaping across streams and slippery stones. Just stop for a second and press a couple of keys to start the basic checks. I jogged on for another 30 seconds then glanced at the display. And had a shock. You know how it is when you're feeling a bit unwell and take your temperature, expecting to see it perhaps slightly above normal and then discover it's nearly up to 40. I'd been expecting a 'clear' or maybe 'possible danger' display. Instead there was the red warning 'great danger', just one point less than the highest warning of 'extreme danger'. I really ought to run some more thorough tests but that would take time, which was in short supply...

I shoved the device back in its case, zipped it up and began to run properly again. Now came the descent towards upper Glen Affric, a mix of bottomless-looking peat and bottomless-looking pools of water, slippery grass and wet rock. I was out of the cloud again, the bleak glen disappearing ahead into the driving rain, a few runners strung out in front. The leaping, sliding, balancing act would have been hilarious had my mind not been otherwise occupied. What was wrong?

The route passes the remote Glen Affric Youth Hostel, around the mid-point of the running stage at ten miles out. A detour across deep peat-hags led to a footbridge over the swollen river, then a fast run up the stony track to the hostel. There were toilet facilities here, I had an idea – I'd probably gained at least five minutes on the next woman and on those men who'd tried to baulk me. It wouldn't take more than two or three minutes to carry out a few more checks on my palm-top.

'Toilets this way!' shouted the helper in reply to my request. Into the hostel, and a door which could actually be locked. Sit down and quickly start typing into my palm-top... yes, there were two portable PCs at the hostel, both infected. Neither looked particularly difficult to deal with; in a few seconds I had links to one via a satellite Internet connection, could download my exorcism software. Repeat with the other. Seconds later the two systems were clean. Check the danger level – blast, still 'great danger'. What on earth could be wrong? No time to find out now. Perhaps things would become clearer during the later stages of the race.

Back out into the wind and rain, I gulped a cup of isotonic fluid and raced off again. I was still the leader of the woman's race but quite a few men had caught up and passed. Ahead, on the left was a new mast. Surely it would not be for mobile phones, out here? Must be. It could be related to the problem, whatever it was but there was no time to investigate.

The rough and stony track climbed up and down along the north side of the valley, I was beginning to feel the effects of the hard run and there were still some seven or eight miles to go. This had become more than just a race though. Blast. Why couldn't I just ignore things and get on with the running – perhaps I should, it wasn't my problem after all.

The rain still drifted across in sheets but was lighter here, more a driving drizzle. It had turned warmer, the warm sector of the front must have come through. Past the next watering station, up and down, and below was the footbridge leading to Altnamullich at the end of the forestry road. Here, I knew, you could get soup, sandwiches, bananas or even Mars Bars from the helpers before the last gruelling six miles to the changeover. A table was laden with goodies under an awning which flapped and rattled in the wind. I can't say I felt like eating, just stopped to gulp another cup of isotonics and grab a banana, long enough to overhear that they were indeed having problems with radio communications. The helicopter was grounded.

Once again came that sickening feeling of oppression and it wasn't just because of dehydration or exhaustion. Stop and investigate? No, carry on, seemed to be the message, push hard!

This last stretch of running, the 'Yellow Brick Road' is

notorious. After miles of rough and wet cross-country the stony surface is hard on the feet and induces cramp in the legs. There are two long climbs and a final mile on tarmac which is the last straw. The scenery is superb but by this stage most are past caring about soaring mountains and a loch ringed with native Scots Pinewoods.

I was running well, ahead of the main pack and amid other fast runners well spread out. A man had been gradually catching me up – then I heard a voice from behind

'Lynne, is it you?'

I looked round.

'Pete! How's it going?'

'Slow! Horrendous conditions back there. You're doing well – if you can keep this up on the bike you'll win the women's race!'

'If,' I said, as we ran along side by side, 'I passed the leading woman back at the Allt Grandda – who was she?'

'That'll have been Susan from Kiltarlity. She won last year.'

'She didn't seem too happy about me going in front...'

We seemed to be pretty well matched for speed so I suggested that we keep together for the next mile or two. Having someone to talk to provided some distraction from the growing pain.

'By the way, what was that new mast just past the Youth Hostel?' I asked.

'Oh that'll be the Hydro. They've automated all their controls for the network of dams and generating stations in the Highlands so that they can be more flexible and efficient in meeting demand.'

'In what way?'

'Well, they've bored some new tunnels to allow water to be moved from one valley to another, they can quickly empty or fill reservoirs, open sluices, switch on generators, all under the control of one or two people. Actually locals were a bit concerned about Loch Benaven, the one we'll be cycling along soon – they reckoned that the dam was old and if all the sluices and valves were opened at once the rush of water might cause it to collapse. It's nonsense of course, all the engineering has enormous safety margins on it, besides there are lots of control and interlocks to ensure that you can't open the lot at once. I know, I was involved in producing some of the software. We actually go past one of the main computer installations in a mile or two.'

'Any software can go wrong!'

'Yes, but there are still manual overrides. Also, the dams are designed to cope with any rush of water, the worst you'd get is some flooding downstream, as happened regularly in the days before the dams were built. There could however be some damage to the generators, so they've made pretty sure that the whole system is robust.'

'Well, I look forward to seeing the loch, especially to getting on the bike ...'

'Mind you don't get cramp. A lot of people find the cycling difficult after the run, so take it easy to start with!'

'Has there been some problem with radio communications?' I asked, as we speeded up for a downhill stretch.

'Don't really know,' replied Pete. 'Certainly the helicopter's not been flying and the RAYNET people seemed to sitting in their tents rather than out with their radios. There could be injuries or exposure cases, too, on a day like this, and with bad communications, rescue could be a bit tricky. I wonder how the Mackenzies are getting on. Some of them will be finding it tough going.... hey, watch out!'

The occasional race marshal had been pottering along the forestry road on a motor-bike or in a Landrover. The white Landrover coming towards us now was certainly not pottering, it was roaring up the hill at about 50 and seemed to be heading straight for us, it WAS heading straight for us, straight for me!

Pete literally dived to the right, heading for a full length sprawl on the track. I leapt off to the left, the vehicle missed me by inches as I tripped and went headlong in the ditch.

The Landrover never slowed and was quickly out of earshot over the top of the hill.

'Are you OK?'

It was another runner who'd been just behind us. Pete had a bloody knee and I'd bruised an arm but otherwise we were lucky, if shaken. We started running again.

'What was that maniac doing. Trying to kill us?'

'Quite possibly,' I said. 'Look Pete, I'm sorry if I sound paranoid, but there's something going on here that's more than just a race. Somebody doesn't want me here, certainly doesn't want me leading the women's race. There's some evil influence at work, too. Something connected with the mast and with the radio communications not working and probably with that woman who won last year...'

Pete groaned. He'd have heard all the tales about me from Norman.

'Can't help you there I'm afraid. Just seems another typically wet "Cross" to me – except for that Landrover. What on earth did he think he was doing?'

We'd now reached the last drinks station, two miles before the changeover.

The track had dipped and a hundred yards on was a white cottage, just off to the side. As we jogged towards it I noticed a couple of Hydro-Board Landrovers parked outside.

'Believe it or not,' Pete began, 'this used to be a bothy; I actually came here 25 years ago to help with roof and window repairs. The estate took it over again a few years later and did it up for wealthy guests. Recently the Hydro-Board bought it for use as their main computer control centre in these parts.'

By now I wasn't listening to Pete. Out of that building emanated a horrible psychic smell, something in there was very bad. O Lord, I thought to myself, what do I do now.

We ran on. The race, the pain of that endless 'yellow brick road', the approaching changeover to the bikes, all were now secondary. Something was badly wrong. A crisis was coming. Like it or not, the outcome would probably depend on me.

In the sheeting rain we jogged up the last hill, now on tarmac, towards the waiting bikes. A few hardy spectators cheered me on, they knew that I was well on the way to winning the women's race. Gradually it was dawning on me that perhaps that was what I'd have to do. If people were trying to stop me from finishing, from winning, there must be a good reason. I'd have to finish to find out!

You can waste a lot of time changing over from running to cycling, what with putting on fresh clothes, eating... but all I did was slip my wet feet out of trainers and into cycling shoes, grab my helmet and set off again. I felt fine on the bike and soon was hammering along the hilly road above Loch Benaven. Midges hung in clouds under the trees, my bare legs swept them up and they kept going in the eyes, ever so often I'd wipe them off before their biting got too bad. Rain alternated between drizzle and sudden downpour. It was warm and muggy. Below, a thunderous roar and a huge white spout of water indicated where a pipe was disgorging into the loch, presumably via one of the new hydro board tunnels. The water-level looked very high, a small tree-covered island was submerged.

I was passing one or two slower cyclists, especially on the uphill stretches, also I'd be overtaken every so often by some real racing cyclist bent low over his extension handlebars. Ahead was the Benaven dam, the water was right to the top and running down the overflow but the outflow river wasn't especially high given the quantity of rain. Below, just across a low wall, roared the Dog Falls, ahead was a steep twisty decent to Cannich, which I knew could be dangerous. I sprinted up a short climb and suddenly felt a sharp pain of cramp in my calf, almost making me come to a halt. Blast – Pete had warned me. As I wobbled up to the crest of the hill, several of those I'd overtaken now hurtled past. At least the downhill would give me a chance to stretch those muscles, a good thing too as suddenly I could pedal no longer, only able to freewheel gently round the bends, foot stuck out at a funny angle as I stretched my leg. The cramp gradually eased off as the occasional fast rider zoomed past at up to 35mph, bike leaning at some crazy angle into the next bend. Here an ambulance was parked, door open, awaiting the almost inevitable casualties...

Suddenly, ahead was chaos. The road was strewn with bikes

and fallen cyclists. I braked hard, I was doing less than 20 but even so the bike slipped from under me and I found myself sliding along the road on my bum, next my head fell back and cracked against the tarmac, thank goodness for my helmet. I came to a stop. There was a strong smell of oil. The road was covered in it.

I picked myself up. A bruised hip but no obvious other damage. Others who'd been going much faster were less lucky, including Pete. Several had nasty, oil-covered grazes. Pete reckoned he'd broken an arm. 'You carry on Lynne, you should still win. I'll go back up the road, warn others and get the ambulance.' There was a yell and a crash as yet another cyclist spun out of control on the oil. Pete jogged back up the road, grimacing with pain. I'd inform the next check-point.

A pedal was slightly bent but otherwise my bike seemed OK. The cramp had simply been forgotten in the panic. But if I hadn't been taking it very slowly I too would almost certainly be out of the race. I set off slowly down the hill again, wondering what might be round the next corner. It looked like another attempt to nobble me...

The road at Cannich was lined with people cheering me on but the sky ahead looked black like the end of the world. Then the heavens opened into a torrential downpour. Damp already, in seconds I was soaked. The road ran with water. Lightning cracked and thunder roared instantly after. 'I'll survive, even if it kills me,' I yelled at the storm and all who were trying to stop me, pedalling harder than ever. Cars were driving slowly, headlights on – except for one. By now I was expecting trouble and wasn't surprised when it made straight for me, crossing the road to run me down – but anyone used to cycling at night knows how to miss a car when dazzled by lights, just aim for the headlight then miss it – which I did, charging straight at that right-hand light then swerving at the last minute just as another lightning bolt cracked nearby. 'Missed!' I shouted at both car and storm, standing on the pedals as the rain became hail, bouncing off the road and turning it a slippery white. My blood was now really up, I'd survive, I'd win, even if it killed me.

The road up Aigas Brae was almost a river, the wind had sprung up from the east and the hail had turned back to cold rain. Nobody had caught me up for a long time, that hiatus in Affric would have held up a few till they managed to spread sand over the oil. Over the top there were still a few hardy spectators cheering in the downpour; then it was down, up, down past the fish ladder and Kilmorack dam. No more attempts were made to stop me, fatigue and the elements were the only remaining obstacles. I hurtled down the hill to the main road, turned left as the policeman stopped the traffic, then the last mile to Beauly and ... The Finish! I turned off the road into the finishing stretch to cheers and claps, the first lady home in just under four hours. Could I get off my bike? Just, I hobbled up to where they were presenting the medals. Now for a shower and a bite to eat, or so I had hoped...but somebody was rushing to talk to me.

'Miss Thomas – sorry to bother you so soon after the race but we desperately need your help. Do you think you could come into the van – we've got a cup of tea for you.' It was the Hydro-Board.

'If you could give me five minutes to change into dry clothes...'

'We've got all your stuff here. You can change in the ambulance.'

True, it wouldn't attract any attention if I disappeared into the ambulance for five minutes, presumably for massage or treatment to a cut. I climbed in, shut the back door. All my dry things were there, it's one of the great things in life to put on warm dry clothes when you're soaked to the skin. The shower would have to wait.

Leaving my muddy wet clothes in a heap, but carefully removing my palmtop, I climbed out of the ambulance and into the back of a waiting Hydro Landrover. Here was a steaming mug of sweet tea, a plate of cakes, sandwiches and a banana. Already I was feeling a new woman. The rain roared down on the roof again, dispersing the crowds outside.

'We're very sorry about having to bother you so soon. I'm Al by the way.'

'Don't worry Al. It's the story of my life. What's wrong?'
I already had some idea.

'We've got major computer problems. All our engineers and experts are trying to sort the system out but we need to get things working soon or we'll be getting into serious difficulty, given the weather conditions.'

'What sort of difficulty?'

'Well, we seem to have lost control of our water distribution network. All the water from both the Monar and the Mullardoch watershed is pouring through the new tunnels into Loch Benaven, in addition to the spate coming down from Affric. We can't close the sluices, they're computer controlled and the manual overrides aren't accessible in the flood conditions. All – and I mean all – the sluices on the Benaven dam just opened about five minutes ago, on their own, we couldn't do anything. Now there's a tremendous flood coming down the glen. We're going to have to evacuate Cannich and all the low-lying houses, there's more water on the way than ever before. But we're concerned for the dam itself, the volume of water pouring over and through it is greater than our design calculations allowed. To be blunt – it might go.'

'The Highland Cross?'

'That's another of our headaches. All the competitors who aren't through yet will be cut off by the flood at Cannich. We're already scrambling helicopter rescue teams but there's a violent thunderstorm up there now and flying conditions aren't good.'

'So – your main control centre?'

'White Cottage, Affric. You passed it at the end of the run.'

Of course. It had been there that I'd known something was really wrong.

'Right, you'd better get me up there as quickly as possible. Presumably you've a helicopter?'

'If you're willing to take the risk. The weather's pretty dire!'

I thought of those still attempting to run and cycle through the storm. A tough lot those Highlanders, though. They'd survive, providing the dam didn't go...

We drove a quarter of a mile through the now drizzly rain to the old Beauly priory where a Hydro-Board helicopter was parked in the grounds, rotors turning. Al leapt out of the van and jogged across to the waiting craft, I followed rather more slowly and stiffly.

The pilot raced the engine and we were off, Beauly slanting off sideways through the haze of rain. Next we were flying up the glen, above the dams.

'I wouldn't vouch for Kilmorack or Aigas dam, either if Benaven goes and a sudden flood comes down the valley,' yelled Al above the roar of the engine, 'we could be heading for a real disaster.'

Below, I could see cyclists still heading down the road towards Beauly and the finish. One of them could be Don, who was aiming for five hours. Ahead, the sky was black, lightning flashed.

'Hold on for a bumpy ride,' shouted Al.

We plunged into the storm. Hail and rain roared against the windscreen. Dazzling lightning flashed. The helicopter dropped like a stone, leaving my stomach behind, then rose again. We carried on, bumping wildly up and down. I peered out of the window.

'Bloody Hell!' I exclaimed. I'm not given to swearing. The river, along which I'd cycled less than two hours before, now filled the whole valley floor. There was Cannich, houses marooned in a flood where people had so recently been cheering me on. The road would be at least a metre underwater.

We bounced and bucketed up into Glen Affric. Where the road ran out of the glen we could see perhaps 150 stranded Highland Cross cyclists on a stretch of road just above the flood. Of course, that would be the Mackenzies. The river, roaring down the steep glen was a frightening brown spate like I've never seen before, well above any natural high level. We flew over Benaven dam, water was pouring over the top, spouting out of every sluice. You could almost feel the shuddering roar of it and, crazily, there were still cyclists heading down the glen. They'd not get past Cannich. Ahead, the glen disappeared into the thick mist of the muggy warm sector weather.

The pilot skimmed low over the muddy brown water of the loch, keeping the shore just in view. We rounded a corner and there was a bustle of cars, tents and people, the Highland Cross changeover.

'He's going to put down here,' shouted Al, 'we'll carry on by Landrover.'

It wasn't a minute too soon for me, I'd been feeling increasingly queasy on the bumpy ride having only just completed four hours strenuous exercise and then been fed on tea and cakes and sandwiches...

We landed next to the grounded Highland Cross helicopter. As we jumped down, ducking involuntarily beneath the still turning rotor blades, a man dressed in waterproofs ran up to meet us. It was Jerry Thomson who was in charge of organising the whole event. There was no radio or mobile phone contact and he was getting very worried about conditions further up the glen for the runners. It didn't take long for Al to let him know that this was the least of his worries, that the glen below was flooded and the dam in a dangerous condition and that nobody else should be allowed to set off down the valley. Jerry put his face in his hands. 'Never again! Let me just organise the Sunday School picnic next year...'

A spare support Landrover was quickly commandeered and we were off again, roaring down the road to the bridge over the Affric, in full spate, then bouncing through potholes and puddles on the 'yellow brick road' back to White Cottage. We were still meeting the occasional bedraggled Highland Cross runner who'd braved the appalling conditions in the mountains.

The bumpy ride was almost too much for my stomach, but I'd survive, even if it killed me, I thought grimly. We reached White Cottage just in time – and immediately a different onslaught on my battered body. Another battle to fight and I already sick and weary... too bad. I'd survive. I'd win.

I put tiredness, even the drizzle and midges out of my mind as we walked up to the entrance and Al unlocked the door. Work, vital work to do. Quickly. Concentrate on that alone.

Al led the way to the control room. Usual semi-circular desk, a couple of computer screens, a big mimic panel map on the wall showing the Northern Highlands with dams and pipes and various lights and flashing colours. A man sat at the desk, typing desperately, there were two others with manuals and a pile of CD roms.

They looked round as Al came in

'Are we pleased to see you! We've lost everything and we're no nearer getting it back.'

'This is Lynne,' introduced Al. 'She's our best hope of sorting the system out. Lynne, meet Jim.' We shook hands.

'Sorry there's no time for proper introductions,' I began. 'If you let me sit at the main console can you take me through what's wrong?'

'The system seems to be running with a mind of its own. If we shut the system down and reboot, it just comes back in the same state. All sluices and valves are open so that everything's pouring into Loch Benaven. All the sluices on the dam there opened, on their own, about a quarter of an hour ago. Apart from the flooding we're very worried about the dam itself.'

One of the bonuses of my job is to encounter a problem which to me is completely straightforward but to others is impossible. To them it appears that I can work miracles. This case looked like one of those, a straightforward possession case, no sign of anything unusually stubborn or especially evil. I pulled out my palm-top, Jim showed me where to connect it to the back of the console computer, and I began to probe. Yes, it was as I'd expected. Probe a bit deeper – suddenly, up on the screen, came a familiar face – it was that lady I'd passed early in the race, last year's winner, Susan Mackintosh. 'You're too late, Lynne, you can't stop us now, revenge is sweet,' cackled a voice from the machine's loudspeaker. Concentrating hard, I only vaguely noticed some surprised reaction from the three men in the room. For me this was pretty mild stuff. Gradually I increased the pressure, the picture shrank, shrank... now the final push. The picture vanished, the screen a clear blue. I set another program in motion to purge any remaining vestiges from the system.

'Right,' I said. 'That should be clear. You should have control again.'

Jim took the driving seat again, clicked the mouse, opened a few windows and clicked again. He looked at the mimic panel.

'Yes, seems OK now. That's the valve from Mullardoch closed... and the Monar valve. Now for the Benaven sluices. He clicked the mouse. He looked at the mimic panel. Puzzled, he clicked again. He opened another window and typed in commands. 'Benaven's not responding!' He tried a few more times.

'We've lost the link to the Benaven dam. We can't control it.'

'Is there another computer at Benaven?'

'Just a small PC, in the building on top of the dam. We always access it remotely from here.'

'Can you control the dam from the PC there?'

' Yes... looks like that's what we'll have to do. Al – you've transport?'

'Yup,' said Al, 'let's go!'

As we bounced back down the track through the driving drizzle, Jim explained that the dam was not designed to operate for long periods of time with everything wide open at once and that the stresses and vibration set up by the volume of water pouring over and through it could, at worst, lead to collapse. It had not been considered credible that a full spate could coincide with a complete failure of control over a long period of time.

'How do we get onto the dam?' I asked.

'It'll have to be by helicopter because of the water flowing over the top.'

'If the dam goes?'

'I'd rather not think about it. Those stranded people we saw, anyone or anything else in the path of the flood, won't stand a chance.'

'You must get them out!'

'We've no radio contact. The dam could go any time. Our first priority must be to close those sluices!'

The helicopter pilot had been instructed to wait at the road-end, ready for take-off with the rotors still turning. We climbed in and just two minutes later were hovering over the dam. A great cataract of water was pouring over the top but still more impressive were five huge spouts of water issuing from the sluices, crashing out with enormous power under huge clouds of spray. In the centre of the dam was a small concrete hut, raised above the flooding water on a small bridge and surrounded by a walkway and railing.

'He's going to hover just next to the railing,' shouted Jim, 'we'll have to jump onto the walkway.'

As the pilot gradually brought the helicopter down to just above the water, Jim opened the door. Spray swirled inside, I could see the railing. Jim jumped. I was next, just a gap of six inches to the railing and, on the other side, the walkway.

I leapt.

My waterproof jacket had been pulled on in a hurry and not properly fastened. It billowed out in the downdraft from the rotor blades and out of the pocket flew something. It was my palmtop. Out of the corner of my eye I saw it sail over the dam and disappear into the spray.

Jim grabbed my arm and hurried me round to the door of the little hut. The roar of flooding and spouting water completely drowned out the rotors of the hovering helicopter. The air was thick with spray. I could feel the whole dam vibrating and shuddering. Inside was a little quieter but felt no more secure. Only the computer equipment on a modern desk gave a feeling of familiarity. I'd have to forget our precarious location and pretend I was in some homely office...

Jim clicked the mouse and the screen lit up. 'No problem with power here, anyway,' he shouted above the roar of the flood. 'Hell, what's this?'

The screen showed, instead of his expected schematic of sluices and generators, a woman's face. It looked a bit like Susan Mackintosh but was much older, lined with sorrow and hate.

'This one's up to me, Jim – but I've lost my palmtop. It may take a bit longer.'

It would. Perhaps too long. Instead of a quick burst of computer power I'd have to deal, face to face, with whoever or whatever was controlling the machine..

'Who are you, what do you want?' I typed.

There was no reply. Instead the picture changed. I saw an old village, high amid grassy pastures. Houses of low stone walls and turf roofs. Small groups of sheep and cattle wandered freely in the midsummer sunshine. Oats and hay grew in little walled enclosures. Nearby, a high waterfall tumbled into a deep glen of alder and birch. I immediately recognised Cul na Skiach falls.

Suddenly the scene changed. Perhaps a hundred roughly dressed men sprang from nowhere. I heard screams. I saw defenceless men butchered by sword and club. Women, young and old, were being dragged off, raped and then murdered. I saw pregnant women being slashed open, I saw babies being grabbed and dashed against boulders, I saw little children tossed alive over the falls to smash to their deaths on the rocks below. I saw houses being set alight, cattle being herded off, crops being trampled. I saw a desolate smoking ruin under the moonlight, I saw an old lady creeping out of hiding in a grain-drying kiln... then she spoke...

'This is what the MacKenzies did to us. Now, at last, we get our revenge. A hundred warriors sacked and burnt our homes. Now a hundred MacKenzies will die in the flood!'

I noticed that the shaking and shuddering of the dam was getting worse. I could hear Jim, as if in a distance, 'Hurry up, Lynne. We can't have long!'

Whoever the old lady was, or had been, she couldn't be right about the massacre. Anything on that scale would be more notorious than Glencoe. Cul na Skiach village was inhabited until the evictions of the nineteenth century. It must have been some more minor skirmish, perhaps when she'd lost her own family, somehow magnified in her mind by centuries of loneliness... but there was no time to argue.

I spoke.

'I don't know your name. I'm sorry. But what happened 400

years ago can't be put right. Today's Mackenzies are innocent, would do anything to prevent such things happening. They too have wives, husbands, children. How can causing yet more pain and grief help?'

'The name's the same. I took an oath that I would never rest till my family, my people had been avenged.'

'So you too will have blood on your conscience? And where will you go when you've done this thing? To the outer darkness? And what about all the other innocents who'll die in the floods you unleash? If you can't forgive you must forget. Today's people can't be held responsible for the past.'

'If your children were killed and your husband murdered in his bed you'd think differently!'

'For nearly a hundred generations my line has faced persecution, torture and death. You know that. Revenge only perpetuates evil. The only hope for this world is forgiveness. We must leave the ultimate judgment to God.'

There was no reply.

'There's still time to save yourself,' I went on. 'Now, I ask in the name of the Father and the Son and the Holy Spirit that you leave this computer and receive the forgiveness due to you. Be at peace with your children.'

The image of the face came back on the screen. She was crying. Gradually it faded and the desktop display appeared.

' Jim, now!' I shouted.

It can't have taken him more than five seconds. A couple of mouse clicks and a typed command and I heard and felt a faint rumble.

'Sluices one and two closed... now for three, four and five...'

The vibration lessened. The roar diminished.

We scrambled out of the door, climbed up onto the railing and were helped back into the hovering helicopter.

The floods were bad, but gradually subsided. All the MacKenzies as well as the other stranded Highland-Crossers were eventually rescued and taken down to Beauly. There had been some problems in the mountains, the later runners had been cut off by floods and spates but anyone competing in the Highland Cross is pretty tough and nobody suffered more than a little mild exposure. Susan Mackintosh had never finished, she'd crashed on the steep descent to Cannich. I never discovered any more about her or those who'd tried to nobble me in the race.

The dam was badly damaged. It had been, at most, minutes away from collapse and the loch had to be drained. It was two years before the reservoir saw operation again.

After a good night's sleep in a Beauly guest house, I'd pretty well recovered. My car started perfectly and I drove out to Boblainy Forest and walked up the old paths above the Bruaich Burn to the Cul na Skiach Falls.

After the deluges, the day was now one of glorious sunshine but the rivers were still high and the falls spectacular. The feeling of oppression had gone completely. I scrambled up beside the falls again and made my way through the recently-felled area to the ruins of Cul na Skiach village. Here too, the feeling was now one of peace, rather than evil. Not consciously thinking, I let my steps be led to one of the low heaps of stones, a long house with the outline at one end of what had once been a circular grain-drying kiln. Something made me lift up a large, flat stone. In a small hollow underneath was a human skull, obviously very old. It was turned face up and there was something about the shape of the bones that I recognised. I replaced the stone. I gathered more stones from the walls and spread them about on top, so that nobody would suspect anything was there. Then, on patch of grass still inside the old walls and next to where I'd found the skull I made a cross of stones. It took, perhaps, an hour in the June sunshine as bees and flies buzzed, as a buzzard mewed from time to time over the muted roar of the falls, as a warm breeze whispered through the clearing.

A great sense of peace descended as I walked away into the quiet trees.